Hope For All Us

Brenda Carroll Jarvis

Golden Street Ministries

Published by:

Golden Street Ministries LLC

547 Georgetown Rd Ext

Brunswick, GA 31523

DEDICATION

I dedicate this book to my Savior, Jesus Christ, who gave me hope

when I felt like there was none.

To my husband, Charles, who sees within me

that which I cannot see.

He believes in my gift, he encourages and supports me

to continue to write what is in my heart.

And to Jordy and Laisha, who inspired two stories.

And, to all those that cheer me on.

CONTENTS

FOREWORD

Every time I have the privilege of hearing Brenda Carroll Jarvis teach or I read one of her books, I come away with a bigger, clearer picture of Jesus.

This new book "Hope for All of Us" is ultimately about God's redemptive affection for all of us.

I was pleasantly surprised at how my spirit seemed quickened to the scriptures. I discovered many things about myself and my relationship with God. It was as if my soul had experienced a renewal and I was left with a sense of excitement for the things of God.

This is the most insightful, encouraging and applicable book about the Bible stories that I have heard for as long as I can remember. Brenda brilliantly took what I knew as a story and made it come to life. She makes the people real. I kept finding myself thinking they are real people who had the same emotions and struggles that I have today.

Brenda takes her knowledge of the scriptures and her gift as a communicator, and her personal relationship with God, to bring these stories to life. She pulls back the curtains of history and suddenly we are weeping with Leah as Jesus loves on her children and provides an unexpected miracle. We rejoice as Ariel takes his first steps. We are amazed when Levi is healed of a dreadful disease and relieved when Hodesh is forgiven and her life is spared. It is easy to follow along with Abigail and Seth as they never stopped praying for their son even though he turned his back on God. In the final chapter, Lucius learns who Jesus really is, as he follows him through his final hours and death on the cross and finally the resurrection.

Enjoy this read. It will bring the Bible to life and strengthen your walk with Christ.

Marsha Bullock

Ordained Minister for 26 years

Children's Minister for 14 years

PREFACE

The stories in this book are dramatized accounts of real events in the Bible. The star characters in these stories are afflicted by various sins, serious health issues, addictions, false gods, weak faith, lack of understanding and even demonic possession.

We all have, at one time or another, been burdened by some of these conditions.

The sparrow featured in the photograph taken by Marcus DiVito of Hubbard, Ohio, reminds us that God cares about the every sparrow, so He certainly cares about us.

These stories by Brenda Carroll Jarvis, of how Jesus changed the lives of Biblical characters, should give hope to all of us, no matter what we face in life.

Jesus is the answer.

*A*re not two sparrows sold for a penny

Yet not one of them will fall to the ground

outside your Father's care.

And even the very hairs of your head are all numbered.

So don't be afraid; you are worth more than many sparrows.

Matthew 10:29-31 NIV

INTRODUCTION

A s I read the Bible, I often imagine the scenes, the people, the conversations, the location and the reactions of those in the story and others who could have been there. These portrayals show the real difficulties, decisions and desperation in their lives. These stories are about men and women who experience transformation through the presence and power of the Almighty God.

In God's Holy Word, there are many stories of nameless people who were witnesses and participants in miracles and demonstrations of God's love and power. They were real people like you and me, who faced difficult situations and perhaps even struggled with their faith. As well as the compassion and presence of the Lord, while God unfolds His plan. Through these dramatized stories, I desire that when you see yourself in the stories, you will realize there is hope for all of us.

The scripture verses that tell of the "The Man at the Gate" were very interesting to me. I thought about him as he sat at the gate. He was there the many times when Jesus came in and out of the temple, yet Jesus did not heal him. His time for healing came after the resurrection and Jesus' ascension to heaven. All the visitors to the temple knew the man as one of the beggars at the gate of the temple, yet one day disciples of Jesus of Nazareth gave him more than silver or gold.

The story of the four men who lowered their dying friend through the roof for Jesus to be healed caused me to wonder how they came together to accomplish getting their friend to Jesus. "Just Hold On" speaks of friendship, faith and the power and compassion of our Savior.

"Discarded Stones" is a familiar story. My heart stirred as I imagined what it was like in that era for a woman caught in an adulterous relationship. The Pharisees used her and the law to try to entrap Jesus to stop his ministry. This story depicts how Jesus delivered a powerful message to her accusers.

"Look Only To Him" reflects the Biblical story of Jesus blessing the children. I envisioned the families that took their children to Jesus. I imagined what these families were facing and what might they have been going through. I wrote the story initially for a real life mother who finally surrendered her family to Jesus and it changed her life.

"Out of the Tombs" speaks about the power of God to break the chains that can bind us, and the importance of not giving up on praying for our children, grandchildren, or others who need freedom through Jesus. It also depicts that demons are real, even in this world today, but Jesus has power over all of them.

In my study of the scriptures about Jesus' crucifixion, and the weeks leading up to it, I was intrigued by the life of the Roman centurion who came to realize that Jesus was the Son of God? He was "The Witness" to the historical event that became the centerpiece of Christianity.

HOPE for All of Us

BRENDA CARROLL JARVIS

Chapter 1

DISCARDED STONES

Jesus returned to the Mount of Olives,

but early the next morning he was back again

at the Temple. A crowd soon gathered,

and he sat down and taught them.

As he was speaking, the teachers of religious law

and the Pharisees brought a woman

who had been caught in the act of adultery.

They put her in front of the crowd.

John 8:1-3 NLT

Hodesh had waited two weeks for today, she had risen early to have plenty of time to get herself ready. She had washed her hair and then put her favorite fragrant oil in her long hair so that it would shine. She pulled out all of her scarves and tried on several colorful ones. She finally decided on one that matched her tunic and robe.

She began to have an uneasy feeling as Achem's arrival time approached. Hodesh walked through the rooms, trying to calm herself as she waited. She listened to the dog's barking, people talking, and the other sounds in the street as she waited for Achem's knock on the door.

For some reason her apprehension increased as she waited for Achem. The time since their last visit had seemed like months, instead of a couple of weeks. She walked through the rooms again and and stopped to straightened the cloth on the table. Then she went into the bedroom to make sure everything was perfect. She looked another time at her clothing to see if it was the right color, she had already changed it three times. She straightened the flowers and moved the fragrant oil from one side of the table to the other.

She was jittery, her thoughts were all over the place, as she paced through her house.

"So why is this so wrong? We are two adults," she asked herself. "The woman that he is married to doesn't support him or care for him. That is why he became interested in me. I know he cares for me, and I care about him," she told herself crossing the room to the window.

Hodesh remembered when she was at the temple, it was a struggle for her to worship God. Her heart would grow troubled as she recalled her actions and her relationship with Achem. Even though she resisted it, she couldn't deny that this was wrong, it was against God's law.

"But, I feel so loved when I am with him, why is that so wrong, God," she said aloud.

Then she felt that pang like at the temple, as she waited for Achem. Hodesh took the scarf from her head and shook it out as if she was shaking off the thoughts that were ruining the excitement of Achem coming. She walked to the window again and looked out, she felt relief when she saw that he was coming down the street. Nervously, she waited for his knock.

Achem was a scribe and messenger for a business in the city. He traveled throughout the Jerusalem, delivering and retrieving documents and messages from businesses and homes. He was neatly dressed and carried a bag for the documents in his care. Achem slowed as he neared the house, looking at each house as if he were looking for a certain place. As he approached the door, he looked around to see who might have noticed his presence. Then he stood at the door, removing the bag from his shoulder, he looked through it and pulled out a document, as part of his disguise and cover for his visit. He held the paper in his hand, and then knocked on the door. Hodesh went to the door and then opened it slowly, Achem stood with the document in hand.

He introduced himself and stated that he had documents that needed her attention. Hodesh responded by inviting him in. Once inside, they knew that time was short for them to be together, there was a sense of urgency with them. It was important not to draw any attention to his visit.

Several moments later, there was a crash at the door, and a group of men, rushed in and were standing at the bed where they lay.

They were Pharisees and temple teachers of the religious law.

Hodesh was shocked and horrified. She began to sob and told them to get out as she covered herself.

Achem got up and quickly dressed.

One Pharisee named Abel took charge, telling Hodesh to get dressed. Abel was in his full rabbinical robes, to indicate that he was there with the blessing of the leadership of the Temple.

Hodesh pleaded with them to leave and said, "Why are you doing this? What does this have to do with you?"

She was in disbelief. She had convinced herself that no one would ever know, find out, or even care. But with the Pharisees and temple teachers of the law finding them, she knew this would involve the whole leadership of the temple. This was very serious. Waves of realization of the gravity of the situation were overwhelming her.

Achem stood with his back against the wall a looked in panic at the men. His heart was pounding his hands shaking. The magnitude of the consequences of his actions was screaming in his head.

He was not afraid of his wife finding out, but this was more than an argument with her. These were Pharisees and the temple's teacher of the law. This meant being taken before the high priest. At the very minimum a there would be a shunning, the worst is a stoning, and it would be his! It was the law, he had been caught, there could be no denying it.

Suddenly, Abel the Pharisee said to Achem with a snarl, "Get out of here! Now!" Abel pointed to the door of the bedroom.

Achem looked shocked hearing the command. He scrambled out of the room as fast as he could. He hurried past the other men as he left the room. He grabbed his document bag and left without looking back.

Hodesh stared in disbelief and confusion, as she heard the leader tell Achem to get out. Then, she saw Achem run out of the house, with no concern for her. He was gone.

She shook as she was trying to dress as fast as she could as the men stood in the room. She repeatedly told the men to get out of her house. The men waited for her to dress. They had a look of disgust on their faces. Hodesh could hardly catch her breath between her sobs and the horror she felt.

The men approached her.

"Wait! Please! Stop! What are you doing? Why, did you let him go?" she shouted at the leader.

Suddenly, one of the Pharisees grabbed her arm and pushed her out of the bedroom. He continued to tightly grip her arm leading her through the front room and then he pushed her toward the front door.

Hodesh tried to fight against the pushing as she yelled, "No, don't do this! Please, I beg you. Don't!"

She reached out trying to grab at something that would keep her in the house. One man moved quickly to keep her other hand from grabbing at the door frame, as he helped to force her onto the street.

Another man grabbed Hodesh's free arm as they began to walk through the streets.

The site of Abel the Pharisee and the men holding onto each arm of Hodesh and the rest of the men surrounding her drew a great deal of attention. Abel looked at the people who stopped to watch their neighbor be taken by the religious leadership. The onlookers shook their heads and then resumed their activities.

Hodesh still pleading and sobbing with the men, asked, "Where are you taking me? Stop! What are you going to do? Tell me! Please!"

She tried to fight to get free, but they held tight to her. Not saying a word, they ignored her desperate questions. She knew that their silence indicated there was a plan.

Abel broke the silence when he asked one of the men, " Did you find out where is he today?"

The man answered, "He is at the temple teaching."

Abel smiled at the man, then pointed in the direction to go.

Hodesh continued to struggle and fight against the men as they pulled her along through the streets. At times as she resisted walking, she would stumble and fall only to be jerked up again and pushed further down the street by the men.

Hodesh grew more fearful with every step, her eyes had a look of terror. Her face was red and tear-stained, and her hands and knees were skinned up from falling. Her tunic had ripped and was dirty from her falling to the ground.

Abel saw their destination, the temple, lay just ahead. He pointed showing the men where to take the woman. They continued to push and pull her as they took her where Abel had indicated. When Hodesh realized where they were taking her, she fought more fiercely. The men were walking directly toward a group of people listening to Jesus, near the temple. Now, they were nearly dragging her, as she fought them while begging and pleading with them. They remained silent to her cries as they approached the crowd.

One of the men pushed the people aside so that the two men holding onto Hodesh could get through. Hodesh didn't stop pleading as they dragged her through the crowd that was surrounding Jesus.

When they arrived at the center of the courtyard with Hodesh, the two men, with a hard push, cast her down in front of Jesus. The ripple of whispers went through the crowd, some pointed at her others gasped. Hodesh heard the words "harlot", "shameful" and "disgusting"being repeated by those in the crowd in the courtyard.

Then the crowd grew quiet, waiting to see what Jesus was going to do. Abel stood looking over the many people that were there. He knew many of the faces.They were merchants, neighbors, and friends.

Yet, Jesus remained silent.

Abel continued to stand with his arms folded over his chest, his men beside him. He looked over the crowd to make sure he had everyone's attention. Then he stroked his beard thinking how best to use this to his advantage.

Hodesh's body was shaking as panic grew within her. She could hear her heart beating in her ears, her mouth was dry. She was trapped. She felt like she couldn't breathe. When she looked up, she saw people that she knew! Even though she felt so ashamed, she mouthed the word "help" to a woman, but the woman turned her head. Hopelessness overcame her, she collapsed in the dirt and covered her head with her tunic.

Then Hodesh heard Abel the Pharisee begin to speak, his voice was loud and clear as he said to Jesus, "Teacher, this woman before you has been caught in the very act of committing adultery."

Another wave of buzzing from whispers was heard as well as muffled sobs from Hodesh. Abel knew that he had the crowd's undivided attention as he continued directing his address to Jesus saying, "In the Law, Moses commanded us to stone such women, what then, do you say?"

Hodesh shrieked, "NO! Please no."

The horror and desperation at that moment took her breath away. She thought, I am going to die, she went limp from the helplessness of the finality of her situation.

Able, with the group of Pharisees and scribes, had orchestrated all of this so that they could have evidence to make accusations against Jesus. He stood trying to hide his smile with his arms folded again while looking down at the woman. He looked to Jesus, and then the crowd.

Jesus stooped down to write something in the dirt with his finger. He said not say one word and didn't look at the men or the people.

Not a sound could be heard in the courtyard, as everyone watched and waited for him to respond.

Several moments passed, the silence of the crowd and the tension was palpable to everyone.

Abel, feeling confident in the plan, repeated the question to Jesus with a tinge of sarcasm as he emphasized the last word, "What say you, teacher?"

After he asked Jesus, he observed the crowd again. Abel never expected what was about to happen.

He saw Jesus stand up. Jesus looked at Abel, then looked deeply into his eyes. Abel sensed that Jesus saw everything that he had ever done in his life. Abel's self-righteousness and pride crumbled in him. He looked down at his feet, ashamed.

Jesus then looked at the rest of the men that came with Abel. They all looked away from his penetrating gaze.

Jesus turned and surveyed the crowd that was silently watching and waiting for what he was going to do and what would happen.

Every person in the courtyard heard the voice of Jesus as he begin to speak with authority.

"He who is without sin among you here, let that one be the first to throw a stone at her."

When he finished his statement, he simply stooped down and again, he wrote on the ground.

The silence remained for several moments. The first sound that was heard was the weeping of Hodesh, then a strange sound of thuds, stones dropping to the ground. Then he heard rustling of footsteps as people left.

The first to depart were the oldest people in the crowd. Then, one by one, they all left, except for Jesus.

Hodesh was still lying on the ground, where the men had thrust her. Her face was covered with the dirty and torn tunic that she held tightly over her head. Hodesh could not hear anyone anymore, yet she was afraid to move. After a time, her weeping began to lessen. With her hands still shaking, she cautiously lowered a corner of the tunic so that one eye could peek out. She wanted to see what was happening. Slowly, she raised her head allowing the tunic to fall completely, uncovering her face. She looked from side to side quickly and she realized that Jesus was the only one there. Everyone else was gone.

Jesus stood and watched her, as she surveyed the empty courtyard. Hodesh tried to absorb what was occurring.

She heard his gentle voice say to her, "Woman where are they, did no one condemn you?"

Now sitting up, Hodesh looked once again to the right and left of her. The people were gone. Even Abel and his men were gone.

When she verified that there was no one but Jesus with her, she responded to him in little more than a whisper, "No one, Lord."

Hodesh stood up slowly, still shaking from everything that had happened. She avoided eye contact with Jesus, still feeling so much shame.

She was amazed when she heard Jesus tell her in a tender voice, but with a tone of authority, "Neither do I condemn you. Go. Leave this life of sin."

Stunned by his words which were full of compassion and forgiveness, she gradually was able to raise her eyes to look at Jesus's face. Immediately she felt peace wash over her at the first glimpse of his face.

As she looked into his eyes they, displayed a love that penetrated deep within her. The love that she felt was holy, powerful, and cleansing.

Hodesh, overwhelmed at the purity of the peace and love from him, closed her eyes to absorb it all. When she opened her eyes she saw that Jesus was smiling at her. Then he nodded to her. When Hodesh saw Jesus's smile, it communicated within her heart and spirit an acceptance, forgiveness and restoration to her. When Jesus turned and walked from the courtyard, she knew that her life was changed by him. Hodesh stood for several moments in the empty courtyard.

She looked all around, remembering all that transpired just a short time ago. She stooped over picking up her tunic and she noticed all the discarded stones scattered in the courtyard. The magnitude of the realization that Jesus had saved her life from certain stoning and death was displayed in those discarded stones.

Jesus used what Abel and his men meant for evil to teach some truths about sin. She began to understand that everyone had sin in their lives, just as she does, and that was when Jesus challenged them to consider if they were without sin. Each person knew that they had to drop their stone and leave. However, Jesus didn't leave as the others did.

Did that mean he had no sin?

Jesus had told her that he did not condemn her, but she needed to leave her life of sin. She remembered the look of compassion that he had when he spoke to her. She desperately wanted a better life, one that did not bring condemnation or judgment. Hodesh knew that she had experienced the forgiveness and love that was from God. She understood that it was powerful and God would show her how to begin a new life.

Hodesh began her walk back to her home through the very streets where she had been dragged, just a little while ago. Her tunic was torn, her clothing was dirty from her being on the ground and her face was tear-stained, yet inside she was free, clean, light-hearted and hopeful.

A smile was on her face she was just beginning to comprehend that she had been transformed by Jesus. She did not doubt that her heart had changed, her mind was clear. Tears began to fall again, not from fear, or panic but tears of joy.

She remembered the words of Jesus, that he did not condemn her. She was clean and forgiven.

While she walked home, she looked at the houses along the streets. She was aware that people were watching as she traveled home. She realized that she would have to face those who lived in those houses and the many other people in her community. It would be difficult because she knew she was guilty of the accusation, but she knew she had been forgiven. She was determined to begin a new life.

The challenge that Jesus gave the crowd in the courtyard, which saved her life, also proved that others were guilty of sins, too. It surprised her how it brought sadness to her heart. She had been forgiven, but did they know that each of them could experience the same freedom? She wondered how she could communicate that message with others.

Her thoughts turned to Achem and his wife.

She prayed as she walked, "Lord help them see there is healing and freedom in you, that is the only way. Bring freedom to them and restore their marriage."

Astonishingly, she realized she felt a love well up within her. Not the shallow, conditional, fleeting kind, but the deep down, unshakable kind. She was beginning to grasp that God Almighty was hearing her prayers. She had never experienced this kind of intimacy with God.

She was surprised that she was smiling and humming again, as she neared her home. As she opened the door of her home, she felt a spasm of remorse about what had happened in those rooms. The depth of what Jesus had rescued her from flooded over her anew. She stood still in the center of the room as peace embraced her, she then said softly, "Fill this place with peace, oh God, like I feel you within me right now."

As Hodesh walked into the bedroom, she felt a surge of energy and determination. She decided that she wanted her home cleansed from the past, she was no longer that woman with those desires. She tore the linens from the bed rolled them up and flung them into the corner. The perfumes, oils, and everything else that was part of her past, she threw in the corner. She took off the torn tunic and the rest of her clothing and tossed them with the linens. She washed herself and put on clean clothing.

To her, it was as if she was removing all the remnants of the past and of sin, to be replaced with all that is clean and new.

She said out loud, "God Almighty, I am burning all of this, I don't want it anywhere in my house."

She stood in her room with her arms outstretched, "God Almighty, I ask that you help me each day to walk faithfully and to be the woman that I saw in Jesus' eyes."

A joy and freedom flooded over her, she started to praise God, and a sense of gratitude began to grow within her. She was singing and praising God for meeting Jesus.

She began to sing:

"If you purify me I know I am clean,

In your eyes, my guilt and shame are not seen

My spirit is restored by your mercy and grace,

My strength is in you for there is no other place.

Your love saved me from a life wasted.

Your peace and joy and love I have tasted.

You saved me from ruin and my place in Sheol.

You touched the inner me and now I am whole."

Chapter 2

JUST HOLD ON

Some men came carrying a paralyzed man on a man

and tried to take him into the house

to lay him before Jesus.

When they could not find a way to do this

because of the crowd, they went up on the roof

and lowered him on his mat through the tiles

into the middle of the crowd, right in front of Jesus.

Luke 5:18-19 NIV

It has been another sweltering day in a week of hot days in Capernaum. Jacob wiped the sweat from his brow as he followed the movements of the crowd through the city.

People have been coming from the surrounding areas to see and hear what this man called Jesus was doing today. Jacob has been curious about Jesus since he arrived a few months ago in Capernaum. He was curious if Jesus was a true prophet, a zealot, or just an excitement that would fade away. Jacob remembered another time, several years ago, when some men made outrageous claims about their special powers, seeking to gain followers. In the end, they were nothing more than showmen.

However, the more Jacob watched and listened to Jesus, the more he was intrigued by him. That evening, Jacob decided to talk with his father regarding Jesus.

"Father, I have been going to the gatherings to see for myself about the man called Jesus," Jacob said.

"Jesus has everyone in Capernaum, and especially in the temple, in an uproar," his father said, in a warning tone. "Did you know that he is from Nazareth? Recently, he went into the temple and read a portion of Scripture then afterwards made some divisive statements and even a prophetic claim."

"I have heard from several people that the temple leaders are amazed at his teachings," Jacob said. "One man who is following Jesus told me that he explains the scriptures with clarity and understanding unlike no one else he has heard. When I heard Jesus speak at a gathering, he spoke of God seeing our sorrow and needs. I have never heard anything like that from a Rabbi."

His father stroked his beard as he listened.

"Well, that might be true. Over the years many of the rabbis have grown lazy in their teaching and care of our people, his father said.

"When people would ask the Rabbis how to draw closer to God, and how to follow God's commands, their answer was only to burden them with rituals, observances of special dates and keeping all the laws.

"Son, I want to warn you; I can only imagine how the priests at the temple are watching him, as well. They will see him as a threat."

"But he has healed people too, father," Jacob said with emotion. "I have watched when people came to him. Some were lame and others were blind. He put his hands on them. I watched their bodies be transformed when they were healed.

"Father, I am watching and studying him. Jesus is different, but I cannot put words to it all. I know that he is unlike anyone else. Do you think, maybe, could Jesus be the Messiah?" Jacob asked, sensing a stirring in his heart.

His father looked at him then peered looked out the window. He did not answer for a moment. Jacob knew that he was sorting his thoughts and his answers.

Finally, after his father shifted a little then answered, "I know that Jesus is unusual and a special man. His ability to heal is amazing, his teaching is unlike any I have ever heard. Furthermore, his character is without question. Now, to say that he is the Messiah, the redeemer, the promised one of God, I do not know, but I can believe that at the very least he is a prophet."

Jacob sat listening to his father and he began to nod in understanding.

"I know you have experienced and seen more than I have. I value your opinion, father," Jacob said. "Each time I listen to Jesus speak, it is as though he knows my thoughts. What the Rabbis are teaching is about the laws of Moses, the things to do and not do. I want to feel close to God like what King David wrote about in the book of Psalms. When Jesus speaks, it is like he is talking about God as a friend. That is what I want."

"I am glad that you are wanting to know and understand more about God for yourself," his father responded. "Maybe Jesus will be a part of it. But I know that God wants each of us to follow Him. I ask that you pray that God will show you what to do. More importantly, you dare to be faithful to what God says."

Later, as Jacob was sitting near the window in his room. He gazed at the stars that had filled the sky. He had remembered the story of his namesake, Jacob, wrestling with an angel all night. He knew he was wrestling in his own heart like Jacob of old. As he was gazing out the window at the deep blue night sky, he began to focus on a particular star and then spoke softly, in part to himself and as a prayer. "God, why did Jacob wrestle with the angel that night? I feel like there is a fight in me, sometimes. I don't even know what the struggle is." His voice drifted off as he was lost in his thoughts as he continued to search for them as he looked out into the night.

Jacob enjoyed living in Capernaum. Generally, it was a busy town. Merchants, fishermen, tradesmen and travelers would come and go. People and merchandise came from near and far on the boats and overland. Capernaum was a hub for people throughout the region to get their supplies, as well as the latest political and religious gossip.

The market square and the temple were full of people nearly every day.

However, when Jesus was in Capernaum there would be larger crowds of people descending on the town. They would swell the streets. Many came from the local region, while others had traveled great distances. Often, they would bring their sick and lame with them. Jesus would speak to the multitudes and heal those who were sick, lame, deaf, or blind.

Everyone in town had an opinion about Jesus of Nazareth. Those opinions were often discussed in the market, at the well and every other place people gathered. The temple leadership watched and listened to Jesus. They wanted to know who he was with, what he was saying and where he was going. They also monitored how many people were believing his message and how they responded to Jesus.

One morning, when Jacob arose, the dawn's light had barely begun to brighten the horizon. He made his way to the fish market. His job was to sort and prepare the catch brought from fishing boats as they came to shore. The market where Jacob worked belonged Aaron, the father of his friend, Levi. He had worked there for the past three years.

As Jacob walked through the early morning streets, he remembered how he and Levi used to work side by side all day long. They talked and laughed as they worked sorting the fish for sale inside the market. He enjoyed working there, Levi was with his best friend.

Everything began to change, Jacob remembered, about a year ago when Levi began to grow unusually tired. Then he started having more difficulty in walking. Soon, it became more difficult for him to come to the market. Levi has not been at the market for months. Now, he is unable to get around at all, he is bed-ridden. Every time Jacob visits him, it is as if there is less and less life in him. He misses seeing the playfulness in Levi's eyes and the jokes that Levi would play on him.

Jacob's father has taken him to several physicians, but there has been no improvement. Jacob was growing more concerned about Levi. He wants to help his friend, but if the doctors haven't been able to help him, what could he do?

The sorting table was just outside of the fish market. There was a separate tent to protect the fish from the sun and weather. Often people would wait near where Jacob worked. He overheard many conversations of the people as they waited to be served at the market. He heard details of upcoming engagements, who was with child and whose mother-in-law was the most difficult to live with. Lately, many the conversations and discussions are about Jesus of Nazareth.

He heard the voice of a woman tell another person, "But, I saw it with my own eyes! I tell you the boy was dead; they were carrying the body out to bury him. When Jesus came by, he reached out and touched the boy, the boy sat up, and he was alive."

Later Jacob heard, two men discussing Jesus' ministry. The younger of the two said, "John the Baptist told us to go ask Jesus if he was the promised one to come or should we wait for another? What do you think?"

The older man said with conviction, "We went to hear Jesus teach, and I know there has been no one before like Jesus of Nazareth."

"Well, we saw the blind having their sight restored, lepers were healed, the deaf heard, the lame walked, and he gave hope to the poor," the young man said.

"John had told us from the start of his ministry, that he came to prepare the way for the Promised One of God," the other man said. "I was there the day that Jesus came to be baptized by John. I remember when John said to Jesus that he was unworthy to baptize him. But Jesus insisted that John baptize him. Afterward, the spirit descended upon Jesus as a dove, and then a voice from heaven spoke saying this was His son."

The men walked away, and Jacob was unable to hear any more of the conversation.

Jacob considered what they had been discussing, the one to come. Were they talking about the Messiah? That question was racing through Jacob's mind as he lifted a basket full of fish to prepare. He remembered the encounter that Jesus had with an official of the town who asked if Jesus could go to his home to heal his son who was dying. Jesus did not go to their home. He told the official to go home and that the boy would be healed.

Jesus healed a boy without touching him or even going to his house, he healed a boy! Jacob repeated in his mind.

As he lifted another basket of fish, Jacob's thoughts turned to his friend Levi. He felt a lump in his throat as he remembered how Levi looked at his last visit. There was no doubt his dear friend was dying. That reality caused a heaviness within him that nearly took his breath away. An idea burst into the darkness of Jacob's despair.

Jacob's face changed from the look of gloom and foreboding, to hope and anticipation.

"After I am done working, I am going to go to Levi's house and talk to him about going to Jesus for healing, " Jacob declared to himself.

The rest of the day, Jacob's mood was brighter. He felt an excitement and a sense of hope as he deliberated how best to present the idea to Levi. He wanted to suggest going to Jesus or having Jesus come to Levi's house.

Jacob's walk to Levi's house was more like a run, as he was eager to talk with Levi. Over the past few hours, he had imagined the conversation by rehearsing what he would say to Levi. Jacob felt a nervousness as he went into Levi's room. Levi was resting on a bed that had been pulled over to the door so he could see outside. The brightness of the afternoon sun was receding from where he lay.

"Levi, are you awake?" Jacob said just a little above a whisper.

Levi answered weakly, "Yes, Jacob, what brings you today?"

"I came to see how you are," Jacob said, as he looked at his friend.

For several minutes, Jacob talked with him about friends and the fish market, as he gathered his courage.

He took a deep breath and then continued, "Levi, have you heard of a man called Jesus, he has been teaching and healing people in town?"

Levi looked at him questioning, "My father has spoken of him to me, saying that he has created unrest among the religious leaders as his crowds continue to grow."

Jacob asked carefully, trying to find out what Levi's father's opinion is on Jesus, "Has your father gone to listen to Jesus?"

Levi thought for a moment, "Maybe if he has, he hasn't told me he has gone. But we have talked about Jesus. Father has mentioned some information about Jesus. I do know that Jesus intrigues him.

"Father has mentioned to me that some think Jesus is the Messiah, but he believes that Jesus is just stirring up the religious leaders. Soon, father thinks, he will fade away."

"I have heard that some think Jesus is the promised of God," Jacob said. "In fact, just today, two men from John the Baptist came to ask Jesus if he was the Messiah."

Levi tried to raise a little on the bed, so Jacob moved quickly and retrieved some pillows and position them behind his back. When Jacob lifted Levi to place the pillows, he felt how thin Levi was. He could see the color of his skin was gray. Jacob tried to hide the shock of his notice of Levi's condition; he knew that his friend was failing quickly.

Levi asked softly, as Jacob moved one of the pillows under his head, "Have you ever gone to hear Jesus?"

"Yes, I have. Jesus is quite different than any other I have seen, Jacob said, encouraged by Levi's question. "When I heard him, he had gone out into a field, thousands followed him and sat down. What was amazing to me was, even though I was with so many others, it was as if he was talking to each one of us."

"What did he talk about?" Levi interrupted.

"Some of what he talked about surprised me. He spoke about those who are meek. It is they, he said, who will inherit the earth. Those that are poor in spirit, he proclaimed that their's is the kingdom of heaven. And those who mourn will be comforted and who are merciful will obtain mercy. He did not talk about the law or how we are breaking it. He talked about the things we face every day. His messages are about issues of our heart." Jacob shared what he could remember.

Levi said, "I have never heard anything like that from the Rabbis, he speaks of the issues of the heart."

Then he added wistfully, "I wish I could go."

Jacob was surprised at his statement; it was as if God had given him the opportunity to present Levi with his plan.

"Levi," Jacob began, trying to control his nerves. "I am so glad, that you said that you would like to go to watch and listen to Jesus. One of the reasons I came today, ...well, um, I came today is because I would like to take you to Jesus, or have Jesus come to you!"

The tone of sadness and defeat in Levi's voice as he answered, hit Jacob hard. "Jacob, my friend, I do not have the strength to go. About Jesus coming here, I doubt my father would allow him to come."

Feeling the defeat for a moment, Jacob tried to think of another way to get Levi to Jesus, he then said, "Levi, I am going to ask God to make a way for you to get to Jesus. If I figure out something, I will come and tell you."

Levi gave a forced smile to his friend then said, "I will wait right here for you."

Jacob returned the forced smile, but he was aware that time was not on their side. He contemplated what he had heard from people who had seen Jesus. If Jesus touched a boy who was dead and brought him back to life, why couldn't Jesus touch Levi and heal him?

With each step he took on the way home, Jacob was more determined to get Levi to Jesus. He considered various options that could allow Levi to hear Jesus and hopefully get close enough for him to be healed.

After several days passed, Jacob could not think of any plan that would work. A desperate feeling grew within him as each day passed. Sometimes Jesus would suddenly leave the area for weeks before returning to Capernaum.

In frustration, Jacob sat on the bench near the window in his room. The evening lamp lights sparkled from the homes, then they dimmed as each family retired. The view from the window grew darkened as the hours passed. Yet Jacob continued staring out his window but not focusing on anything. His thoughts went one direction then another, while he deliberated on how to help Levi encounter Jesus.

A deep long sigh escaped Jacob, as he lingered at the window. His heart was as dark as the homes outside the window. Several yawns urged him that the hour was late. It was time for bed. He thought of

Levi as he pulled down the covers of his bed. He knew that Levi was lying in his bed, but Levi's bed had become his prison.

More determined to find a way, he was still struggling to find a solution, he drifted to sleep.

The next morning, at the fish market, he dumped a basket full of fish on the big table to be sorted. The large wooden table had a flat surface with small holes to allow the water to run out. The sides around the table were to keep the fish inside the table and not to slide off or flop out. There were four men positioned on each side of the table, each assigned a type and size of a fish. When the fish were sorted, they were put in tall baskets that were immersed in water beside them. The men discussed topics every day while they worked, from the food that was cooked at home to the news from the area.

Jacob asked the men as innocently as possible, "Have any of you listened to the man Jesus of Nazareth, since he has been in town?"

The three men around the table, Nathan, Benjamin and Daniel, at first looked at Jacob not saying a word.

Jacob began to wonder if he should not have asked the question. He was trying to think of something else to say.

"I have gone to listen to him, he has an interesting way of telling you about God," Daniel said timidly."

"The other day, Jesus healed a man with leprosy," Benjamin added. "I must be honest; I was shocked. Jesus was not afraid to be near him or to even touch the man. After Jesus touched the man, at once, the sores were gone. The man began to shout and praise God. Jesus told the man to go to the temple to have him be declared clean. Honestly, Jacob, I keep thinking about Levi." Benjamin added.

Jacob's heart leaped. He wanted to tell them that he was trying to find a way to get Levi to Jesus. Something stopped him, and he remained quiet.

Then there was an awkward silence around the table for a few moments. Then Daniel poured another basket of fish on the table, and the sorting began again.

"I watched him one evening, just outside of town," Nathan offered. "There were people everywhere. Some that were there had all kinds of sicknesses. Jesus touched them one by one; they all were healed."

"It was obvious that the people were sick. Jesus undoubtedly healed them. I recognized some of them, and I know that a few have been sick for a long time," Nathan said, as he tossed a large fish into the basket on his right. "Jacob, I am glad you said something about Levi. How can we get Jesus to him?"

Jacob quickly replied, "I was just with Levi yesterday; I spoke with him about seeing Jesus. He does want to see him, however, he is too weak now. He can no longer get out of bed. He believes that his father will not allow Jesus to come to his house."

"We need to plan something; I am fearful that our dear friend Levi has no other hope for recovery," Jacob said, looking to his friends around the table.

They all promised to try and think of a way to get Levi to Jesus. As they continued working, there was a more somber mood among them. They knew their friend Levi was in dire need of healing.

Several days passed as Jacob sought more information regarding where Jesus would be in the area. He needed to know, in advance, when and where Jesus would be. Lately, he would only find out where Jesus had been. He was always gone before he could get Levi to him. Now, he was desperate to know where he would be before he arrived or while he was teaching so that he could try to bring Levi.

As Jacob and his father sat at the table with the evening meal, his father noticed that Jacob was greatly distressed the said to him, "Is there something wrong? Are you sick, have you lost your position at the fish market?"

"No, no, there is nothing wrong with me, it is Levi," Jacob's voice broke with emotion. "Every time I go, he is weaker, he is confined to bed now. He is so frail. I am worried about him."

His father could see the concern Jacob had for his friend and said, "Son, I understand how difficult it is to see Levi in such a condition. I am so sorry. I should go to visit his father. I cannot imagine what he is going through. He must feel so helpless to watch his son go through this."

Jacob's head jerked up as his father finished speaking then asked, "If you go, can you talk to his father about taking Levi to Jesus?"

"Jacob, I do not believe that is my place, to interfere in that way. Jesus' presence in town and his ministry has provoked many people. I am not sure what Aaron thinks of Jesus."

"But, father, if it were me, would you take me to Jesus?" Jacob asked.

His father was surprised by Jacob's question. After thinking for a moment, he said. "I can only speak for myself, I know I would do everything possible, even taking you to Jesus. If there is an opportunity to speak of it, I will see if Aaron will listen."

Jacob was awake again through the night, as he remembered his conversation with his father. He asked himself some questions to clarify his thoughts. What do I believe about Jesus? Do I really believe that my friend will be healed? Do I believe that Jesus is the Messiah? Did God Almighty send him? If he was not sent by God, then by what power does he do these miracles?

A gentle voice spoke within his heart, "Do you believe God cares about every part of your life like Jesus shared? Do you trust in God? Who do you think Jesus is?"

Then Jacob's thoughts swirled around. Once again he was wrestling with surrendering to God or just living his life the way it came. He could not escape the peace he had, when he would listen to Jesus speak. That peace was pure and sustaining.

Jacob's battle within his heart continued all night long. He said, within his heart, a prayer, "I want Jesus to be from you, God. I realize I want all that Jesus has spoken about."

Jacob felt comfort as he finished the prayer. He drifted to sleep and rested for the first time in weeks.

Jacob awoke, and immediately decided, that he would go out in search the town for Jesus. He needed to find out where he was teaching. Grabbing the bread from the table, he headed out the door and walked toward the temple.

Near the temple, Jacob noticed a group of local priests walking, and along with them were other religious leaders unfamiliar to him. He noticed by their dress that some came from Jerusalem, others from Galilee, Judea and the surrounding areas. Jacob was aware that that the local priests were constantly monitoring where Jesus was teaching. He was sure Jesus was in town, but where?

Urgently Jacob rushed to the temple to see if Jesus was there. Then he raced to the places where Jesus had taught previously. He began to run toward the home of a follower of Jesus. As he drew closer to the area of the home, he saw a few people who were bringing a lame man and a sick boy. Jacob knew he was close, crossed the street and noticed people were gathered outside of the home. Some stood at the door, others at the windows. He had found where Jesus was!

Jacob knew he had to hurry, he raced through the streets, dodging carts and groups of people as he ran. Arriving at the fish market, he goes into the sorting area for his friends. Stopping for a moment to catch his breath, his friends looked at him in wonder.

Jacob still breathless, said in a commanding voice, "Nathan, Benjamin, and Daniel. Come quickly, we have little time, I found where Jesus is! We must go for Levi, now!"

The men were startled at first. Daniel said, "Let's go!"

They had taken off the aprons and followed Jacob. Instantly, they were running through the streets to Levi's house. When they arrived, Jacob was stunned to see his father, Micah, there. He was there talking to Aaron, Levi's father.

Aaron and Micah saw the four friends arriving, each one trying to catch their breath. They both questioned what was happening. Jacob excitedly explained that Jesus was teaching at one of his follower's homes nearby. Jacob cleared his throat, then asked Levi's father, if he and his friends could carry Levi to where Jesus was teaching, with the hope of him being healed.

Aaron studied Jacob and the three friends. His face could not hide his emotion. Jacob could see his agony, fear and helplessness for his son.

"We will carry Levi on the bed with care, Jacob said. We don't want any harm to come to him, we only want him to be healed and restored."

Aaron responded with tears in his eyes, with a nod, then led them to the Levi's room.

Aaron said to his son, "Levi, your friends are here. They want to take you to see Jesus, is it your wish to go?"

Levi spoke as loudly as he could, "Yes father, but how?"

The friends entered his room, full of excitement and determination to get Levi to Jesus.

"Ready, Levi?" Jacob pled.

Levi nodded and smiled.

Daniel and Nathan wrapped Levi in blankets. Benjamin and Jacob used ropes to secure him to the bed.

Aaron watched the four men, who carefully and lovingly prepared his son to take him to Jesus.

The friends moved quickly, yet as smoothly as possible, through the streets to the place where Jesus was teaching. When they arrived at the destination, there were so many people gathered outside the house. The whole street was filled with people, creating a barrier for them to get close to the front of the house. It would be impossible to get inside this way.

Levi's bed was set down for the friends to rest a moment, and to figure out a way to get through the crowd to Jesus.

As Nathan and Benjamin looked at the crowds, the look of defeat shone on their faces.

"We believe, we arrived too late, just look at the amount of people outside. How are we to get Levi in? Daniel said. "How can we get past all these people."

Levi heard them, with that forced smile said weakly, "Thank you for trying to help me, my friends. At least I have been able to go outside."

Jacob held up his hand to tell them to stop talking.

"Are we going to give up so easily?" Jacob asked. "Jesus is right over there, in that house!

Yes, we know that there are hundreds of people in the street, yet I am confident that God will show us what to do and how," Jacob said firmly, as he began to silently call out to God to do something, quickly.

A look of inspiration came on Daniel's face. "Wait here, I'll be back," he said. Not waiting for any response, he then ran around the corner. Jacob looked at Nathan and Benjamin with questioning in his eyes. They waited to see what Daniel was going to do.

Daniel returned quickly, with a huge smile on his face, and looked at Levi, then said to Jacob, Nathan, and Benjamin, "I think I see a way to get him in, but we have to move fast."

"Let's hear it, my friend," Jacob said.

They all listened as Daniel explained an interesting plan to get Levi inside the home where Jesus was. Daniel cautioned them saying that speed and focus were imperative.

Daniel then asked Levi, "Are you in agreement with this Levi? Do you agree with our plan? We are going to do our best to be gentle with you, we know that you will have to trust us completely."

Levi looked at his friends, a smile crossed his face, with a hint of apprehension he said, "What are you waiting on, let's go!"

They lifted the bed and rounded the corner to the side street. The four friends carefully lifted Levi out of the bed, then wrapped the blankets around him, then bound ropes around his chest and his hips. Then ropes were tied to the ropes that were around his chest. Daniel and Nathan climbed up first to the roof of the home.

Jacob bent over Levi and said, "Just hold on my friend."

Levi said to Jacob, swallowing his emotion, "Thank you, Jacob, no matter what happens."

Benjamin threw the ropes up to Daniel and Nathan then he climbed to the roof.

Jacob stayed with Levi, as the three men began to pull on the ropes. Jacob steadied Levi, ensuring that he did not hit the side of the building as they pulled him up to the roof of the home.

Once Levi was on the roof, Jacob climbed up too, Daniel went quietly and quickly to a section of the roof over a large room of the house. He returned and told them that the roofing would be easy to remove. They carried Levi over and placed him near where they would make an opening.

Jacob's heart was racing. He began to think, what if we do all of this and Levi is not healed, and he dies? What if people think we are crazy? Lord God, please give Jesus the power to heal Levi, his heart begged of God.

Daniel, Benjamin, and Nathan rapidly began to grab and remove the layers of palm branches that made up the roof over the patio. As soon as they began, people began yelling for them to stop, as debris fell on the people below. The four friends did not listen to the people's protests, as they focused on their goal, get Levi to Jesus.

Nathan gave Jacob a wave and a look that said they were done. Daniel got up and helped Jacob move Levi closer to the hole.

Jacob rechecked the ropes that held Levi, confident of his safety, then said, "Are you ready?"

Levi could hear the people continuing to yell at them, he looked at Jacob with tears filling his eyes, then smiled nervously and said "Yes."

The four friends carried him to the opening, then began to cautiously lower him feet first into the room where Jesus was.

The people in the house stared and then grew silent as they watched a mat being lowered through the opening with a man tied to it. They lowered it slowly so it would not swing. Some of the people moved from their place, making room for the man in the mat. The foot of the mat slowly and softly touched the ground, followed by the head of the mat.

The men let go of the ropes, once Levi was safely on the ground, then they laid on the roof, peering through the hole to watch what would happen.

Levi tried to keep calm, as he was being lowered. He felt excitement, apprehension and fear. He wanted desperately to be healed, what if this didn't result in his healing then what would he do? The first thing he saw were the shocked look on the faces of those looking at him. Immediately, he began to search the room for Jesus.

Once on the ground, Levi realized that the excitement of trip from his home to this place, had left him feeling very weak. Levi panicked, he was unable to loosen the ropes over his chest.

He turned his head from side to side. He looked at the all the people that gathered in the home. He was trying to find Jesus, but having never seen him, he didn't know how to identify him.

Levi noticed a man seated near him. The man was looking up intently at his friends above, who were looking down. Levi then glanced up to his friends, then he saw Jacob pointing to the man seated near him and nodded. Levi understood that man was Jesus!

Jesus looked up and smiled at the men above him. He stood up and moved closer to Levi. Jacob watched as Jesus looked at Levi, then said to him, "Your sins are forgiven."

Everyone present reacted, as people gasped or commented to the people around them. The noise of the people was surprising as they reacted to Jesus' statement.

Immediately the teachers of the Law and the other religious law-keepers who were seated near Jesus were taken aback.

"Who does this man think he is, he is speaking as if He was God? Only God can forgive sins," one of them muttered.

Jacob was closely watching Levi, Jesus, and the religious leaders.

As Jesus turned to the religious teachers and leaders. He spoke to them directly revealing that he knew exactly what they had been thinking.

"Why do you think that way in your hearts?" Jacob heard Jesus say to them.

Jacob could not take his attention off of Jesus. He could see an intensity in Jesus' eyes that was challenging them. Then Jesus asked them, "Which is easier to say, your sins are forgiven or to get up and walk?"

Jacob was stunned, he could not only see but feel the conflict between the religious leaders and Jesus.

Jacob observed the reaction of Levi, as Jesus and the religious men spoke. Jacob was concerned, he had promised that he would protect Levi. He noted that Levi didn't take his eyes from Jesus, even though Jesus' statements were to the men near him.

Levi knew from conversation with his father that the religious leader opposed Jesus and tried to disrupt his ministry at every opportunity. In the midst of that Levi felt that Jesus had a holy power. At the same time, as Levi remained focused on Jesus, he sensed a love wash over him that was refreshing and soothing. He knew it came from this man that stood so near him, Jesus. The love that came from Jesus brought so much calm that Levi just closed his eyes, allowing the immense love to bring peace.

Jacob, not moving from his spot on the roof, watched Levi close his eyes! Did he go to sleep or did he...?

The voice of Jesus drew Jacob out of his thoughts, he looked down to the scene below.

While looking at Levi, Jesus said, "So that you know, the Son of Man has the right and the power to forgive sins. I say to you, get up, pick up your mat and go home."

Jacob watched Levi, to see what was going to happen. He glanced at his friends, then back to Levi.

Levi eyes were big as he listened to Jesus spoke directly to him. At the command by Jesus to get up, to take his mat and go home, Levi felt a surge of power go through his whole body. It was as if his body had reacted to the voice of Jesus. Levi responded to Jesus' words, he was able to move his arms. He quickly loosened his ropes from his chest and hips.

Something inside of him gave him confidence that he had the strength to stand. He stood with ease. He could barely contain the joy he had as he felt strength in his whole body. He looked at his shaking hands, he touched his legs, and arms. He took a couple of steps. He felt no weakness, the fatigue was gone! His mind was trying to catch up to the change in his body.

He looked at the mat and the ropes on the floor, he could feel a surge of gratefulness begin to overtake his emotions. He was no longer confined to a mat, he had been set free. His voice was a whisper as he turned to Jesus, he wanted to say something, but had no words that would express the gratitude that he had. Jesus looked at Levi then nodded at him. Jesus had a sparkle in his eyes when looked at him. It was as if Jesus knew exactly what Levi had in his heart and what he wanted to say to him.

Levi was filled with peace. He bent over and rolled the blankets that had been his mat and put it under his arm,. He looked at Jesus with a feeling of awe and gratitude that overflowed his heart, soul, and mind.

While Levi moved through the people, to make his way out of the house, he scanned the faces of the people that were looking at him. He saw the faces of people that he knew and of a few neighbors. With smiles and tears, they were all able to see the joy that he was experiencing.

Levi stopped for a moment, to absorb the reality that he was standing and walking on his own. He realized that he felt unburdened, clean and forgiven.

As he moved through the crowd, Levi's voice finally began to have sound. He kept repeating, "Glory to God, Blessed be the Name of the Lord, you are my Jehovah Rapha! His voice grew from a whisper to almost a shout."

Finally, Jacob reached Levi as he found him in the crowd. Jacob hugged him tightly, and he kept saying, "Jesus healed you, you're healed!"

Nathan, Benjamin, and Daniel were just steps behind Jacob, each rejoicing in Levi's healing and hugging him.

The men were unable to speak or to contain the wonder, joy and relief of Levi's healing.

Each step of their walk toward Levi's house was full of emotion and celebration. As they accompanied Levi home, Nathan, Benjamin and Daniel went on to their own homes, excited to share their experience with their families.

Jacob waited to watch, as Levi opened the door of his home. He went directly into the arms of his father.

Aaron stepped back from his son to scan him from the top of his head to his feet. Tears streamed freely from Aaron's eyes as he looked at his son who had been restored to health, no longer frail and near death. Levi stood before his father, strong, healthy, and praising God.

"Jesus healed you. What did he do? Aaron said through sobs as he kept hugging him repeatedly.

Aaron motioned for Jacob to come in, then he turned from Levi and said with a hoarseness to his voice, "Jacob, what can I say that is more than thank you? You gave me my son back!"

Jacob waved his hands in protest, then answered quickly, "No, no! I did not heal him. It was Jesus, not me."

Again, Jacob thought, Jesus healed him without even touching him. So where did his power come from? Is he the Messiah? Had God sent him?

He remembered what Jesus said to the religious leaders and the crowd. So that you know, the Son of Man has the right and the power to forgive sins. He told Levi to get up, pick up his mat, and go home. Jesus forgave his sins, and then he healed him. Jacob remembers that part, "so that you know...," he wants us to know, to have no doubts.

Jacob heard Aaron clear his throat and softly asked, "Can you tell me about it? What happened?"

Aaron wanting to know every detail, looked over to Jacob and then asked, "Tell me everything, how you saw it, Jacob."

Jacob was sitting at the table, looked to then Levi then said, "We were so eager to take Levi to where Jesus was teaching. Honestly, I was disappointed when we arrived the house where Jesus was. We found that the street was impassable, there were so many people. The access to the house, to Jesus, was impossible. I did not know what to do.

Levi added, "Daniel left us to find another way in, which he did!"

"He found a way to the roof of the house where Jesus was teaching. Daniel had a most unusual plan," Jacob added.

Excitedly Levi said to his father, "It was to remove the palm branches and supports from the roof. Then they lowered me into the center of the room."

Aaron sat smiling and listening to them as they shared the telling of the miracle.

"When Daniel suggested lifting him to the roof and lowering him down through the hole, I knew this was the only option for Levi," Jacob said with conviction.

Then, almost laughing, Levi said, "Jacob told me 'Just hold on!'"

"I'm glad I didn't see that!" Aaron said grinning at Jacob, even though tears still brimmed in his eyes, and joy was evident on his face.

"Father, they had me wrapped in the blankets and they tied the rope tightly, I knew that I was safe," Levi said.

Aaron listened as Jacob continued, "The four of us removed the palm branches and the supports, then we lowered him into the middle of the room. When small things fell on the people, they started yelling at us to stop. I could see everyone watching us, they had no idea what we were going to do. I saw Jesus look at each of us and he smiled! To me, it seemed like he looked into my heart.

"I looked then to Levi. I saw that he was looking to find which man was Jesus. I signaled that Jesus was right beside where we put him on the floor!"

"Father, you could feel his power!" Levi broke in. "And he had a love that I don't know how to describe."

Jacob then reminded Levi, "Tell your father, what was the first thing Jesus told you?"

Levi's said to his father with trembling in his voice, "He told me that my sins were forgiven."

Aaron looked at Levi then at Jacob confused, then said, "What? Why?"

Jacob then commented, "There were many religious leaders there. I had seen them earlier this morning going to the house. They are frequently present wherever Jesus is. They scrutinize everything about him, what he says and what he does."

"When Jesus said that my sins were forgiven, the look of anger in the eyes of the religious leaders was startling, Levi said. "Jesus said to them 'So that you know the Son of Man has the right and the power on earth to forgive sins.'"

Pointing to himself, "Father, He said to me, 'I say to you, get up! Take your bed and go to your home.'

"Oh, I wish I could explain the power and the peace that went through my whole body when he said those words. I remember I had the thought that I needed to loosen the ropes, and immediately my body obeyed! I could move easily. I loosened the ropes without thinking and when I stood up, it was as if I had never been weak or sick.

"Father, I felt stronger than I ever have been in my life. I bent over and rolled up the blankets and the ropes. Then Jesus smiled at me. I have no doubt He is the Messiah. I have never felt the presence of God like when I was with Jesus, I can still feel it.

"I want to tell you, when he said to me that my sins were forgiven, I instantly felt peace and freedom. It was as if a weight lifted from me. I had not realized how heavy my heart was until he said I was forgiven." As Levi finished, his the brightness and smile mirrored his words.

Jacob stood up and said "Aaron and Levi, I must get home. I know my father is waiting for me. I am excited to share this all with him. Aaron, patting Jacob's shoulder and trying to control his emotions said to him, "We will come by later. Thank you."

Jacob began his walk home, as the day's events replayed in his mind. Jacob remembered the moment when Jesus looked up to the hole in the roof and saw him. He knew he could see it all, the questions, the struggles, the hurts and the losses. The presence of God and his authority and peace returned to Jacob as he remembered that moment. Jacob was grateful that he had reached the door of his home because he became aware his cheeks were wet from tears. When he entered the home, he saw his father there waiting for him. Jacob went to him and embraced him.

"Oh, father, Levi was healed!" Jacob said, as the emotions of the day came pouring out. "What an incredible thing to witness! Jesus is the Messiah; I know, there is no doubt! When he looked at me, I knew. Everything he has been saying and teaching came from God."

His father watched and listened to Jacob tell of the crowded street, finding another way in, of lowering Levi through the roof and of Levi's healing.

"Levi got up, picked up his mat and walked home under his own strength," Jacob said, displaying his amazement.

He knew that the questions he had about Jesus had been settled.

Jacob sat with his father for the rest of the day. At times he was emotional, reliving the day's events. He shared with his father the impact on him when Jesus looked at him and the power he felt when Levi stood up.

As the long shadows gave way to the glow of the evening sun rays, Micah continued to sit with his son talking. They had not had a time like this for a long while.

Jacob shared how he had been wrestling with God.

"Father did you ever struggle with God? I desire to be close to God, but there is a battle inside me."

As Micah looked at Jacob his heart overflowed with love for his son. He remembered tender moments with him as he grew. Now, he was viewing his son in a new way. He saw his courage, determination and passion for those that he cared about. He also saw that Jacob had a longing to know God more deeply.

Micah put his hand on his shoulder and responded with a huskiness to his voice, "Oh son, I remember, many times when I had spent night after night wrestling with God. I had to face myself and allow God to reveal himself and his plan for me.

"I have learned over the years that God will allow us to wrestle with him if our hearts are open, and we have a yearning to draw closer to him," Micah said. "I believe you have seen, as you have struggled, whether or not Jesus is the messiah. Yet, God used this experience with Levi to prove that he does not stop loving us, or seeking us to be in relationship with him, even when we may not be seeking him."

Jacob listened intently. "You are right," he said. "I knew, I had to get Levi to Jesus, something kept pushing me."

"God was able to reveal to you that Jesus is the messiah, through your desire for Levi's healing," Micah said. "Look at how you needed God to guide you at every step of the way. You prayed for God to make a way, didn't you?"

"But what do I do now, father? Jacob asked. "I want to be like David; he was so close to God. When I read what he wrote, I see that he knew God more deeply. That is is something I want."

His father said to his son with love, "Give in to God, stop resisting His love and presence. Hasn't God been revealing himself to you through Jesus and his teaching and greatly through Levi's healing?"

"Son, talk to him the way to talk to me. You will never regret it, my son, I never have."

More relaxed now, Jacob smiled and said, "Yes, Jesus must be the Messiah. He had to be sent by God!

"Thank you, father, I know what to do now. When we raised Levi to the roof. I asked Levi to trust me. I wanted the absolute best for him. I knew that he was dying. I knew what I was doing was for his good and not to harm him.

"As I have talked with you, I remembered something that Jesus said, 'So that you know.' He wants me to know without a doubt he is with me. That is how God loves and cares for me. He wants me to trust him totally, I realize that I need to trust God, and just hold on."

Chapter 3

THE MAN AT THE GATE

"When he saw Peter and John about to enter,

he asked them for money. Peter looked straight at him,

as did John. Then Peter said, "Look at us!"

So the man gave them his attention,

expecting to get something from them.

Then Peter said, "Silver or gold I do not have,

but what I do have I give you.

In the name of Jesus Christ of Nazareth, walk."

Acts 3:3-6 NIV

A riel was trying to hurry to be ready when his brothers would come for him. Still, he could hear his brothers, Nathaniel and Laban, complaining that he was taking too long to get ready.

Why couldn't they understand that it took longer for him to do everything?

Nathaniel shouted at Ariel, "Look, Laban and I need to get you to the temple. We have other things to do!"

Ariel finished his small piece of bread and cheese without saying a word. He looked up to his brothers with an empty look on his face, and with the same emptiness in his voice, he said to them, "I'm ready."

Laban glanced at Nathaniel and then said under his breath, "About time."

Nathaniel brought the netting and pole over to where Ariel was seated. The pole went through the netting at the top, then the lower bottom section was placed behind Ariel. Rocking from side to side Ariel worked the coarse netting under himself until it reached his knees. Ariel then used a rope to gather the sides of the netting to make a seat.

Ariel held the netting tight and then said to them, "Ready."

Laban and Nathaniel stood on either side of Ariel, putting the pole across the back of their shoulders, then they stood, lifting Ariel from his place. As they gained their balance, they took a couple of steps as they adjusted the poles and weight on their shoulders. This jerking of the pole into place caused Ariel's seat to swing hard from one side to the other several times.

Fearing he was going to fall out, Ariel held on tighter. He knew better than to say anything to them. They detested carrying him to the temple every day. He knew from the past that if he complained, it would only make the trip to the temple worse. Ariel held on tight and prayed he didn't fall out of the seat.

Ariel was born with feet that were turned to the inside and hung limply, making it impossible to walk. For the past forty years, each day he was carried to the temple to beg; he sat alongside the many others who were lame, blind an ill.

Day after day, and year after year, this trip was made. Regardless of whether the day was hot, cold, or rain, it didn't matter. Ariel was taken to the Gate Beautiful to beg alms. He sat at the same spot, with the same beggars, and watched the same people come and go to the temple. Those who came to the temple were the rich, the poor, the teachers of the law, the rabbis, and the priests. He noticed when someone would travel from a far distance and knew those who lived nearby.

The other beggars that were at the Gate Beautiful, many of them, had been there for years, just like he had. The best places to be seated are the ones closest to the gate entrance; those spots provide the best chance to receive attention and alms. Those furthest away received little attention. Ariel's spot was one of the best. He had acquired that spot because of the number of years he had been going to the gate. The only time a beggar can be moved closer to the entrance is when a beggar with a closer spot dies or stops coming.

Over the years while he sat at the Gate Beautiful, he observed the lives of families. He watched as a couple would come with a baby to be dedicated, then a few years would pass, then see that baby grow to have the Bar Mitzvah. Soon that child would grow into an adult, then bring their baby to dedicate. Even though he recognized the people who came to the temple, he was often invisible to them. In spite of the fact that there would be coins tossed at him, no one looked at him as a person. No one would talk to him. He felt like an object. He was a part of the temple, like the pillars or the planters. He was not seen as a person; he was just a fixture of the temple.

During the long hours that he sat at the gate, he would often hear the conversations among the leadership of the temple. Repeatedly, he would hear the gossip of the temple as the rabbis stood at the gate. Other times, the men of the community would stand near where he was seated and discuss the problems and people of Jerusalem. They never noticed that he was there. Because of that, he had heard intimate details of the lives of people and their families. Some of the information was shocking, other information was heartbreaking. Other times there was the harsh judgment of the people with whom they were having the discussion.

However, over the past few years, for Ariel it has been more interesting at the gate. The man from Nazareth called Jesus has stirred up the religious leadership. Jesus has become the topic of most conversations for the Rabbis, community leaders, shopkeepers, even the common people of Jerusalem, as well as the visitors from afar. Everyone has something to say about him. His message, travels, activities, and even those he dined with were discussed by everyone. It seemed that most people had an opinion about Jesus and shared it freely with anyone who would listen. Most of the rabbis openly criticize him as a heretic and a threat because Jesus healed on the

Sabbath, touched lepers and he even stopped the stoning of a woman caught in adultery.

Ariel would then be astounded by other people who came to the temple praising God and Jesus for their healing. He was shocked when a man called Lazarus came to the temple and declared that Jesus had raised him from the dead after being dead for four days. Those with Lazarus said that they had witnessed it. From that point, Ariel watched and listened more intently to the news or information about the man called Jesus of Nazareth.

Ariel knew that when Jesus was in Jerusalem, the activity at the temple greatly increased. It seemed as though more and more people were coming from areas further away, some as far north as Nazareth. The increase in people at the temple was beneficial for the beggars in terms of the amount of alms received in a day. Even though Ariel was intrigued by Jesus of Nazareth, he did not have any strong opinion on whether Jesus was a heretic, a zealot or a prophet. He was aware that the activity around Jesus coming to the temple helped to pass the time that day and often helped to fill his cup for alms.

Ariel could tell that the leadership of the temple was becoming more aggressive in its attempt to stop Jesus' influence. Caiaphas and his men would speak frequently near where Ariel could hear their conversations and plans regarding Jesus. Caiaphas was sending men to watch and listen to Jesus, then report back to him.

Then, at Passover, the temple leadership and high priest were able to have one of Jesus' followers provide information about his location so that the high priest and temple leadership could have him arrested on some falsified charges.

Every time that Ariel thought of those days, he would shiver; it was horrible. Jesus was arrested in the dark of the night and taken to Caiaphas, where he was beaten and then taken to Pontius Pilate. Even though Pilate found no crime in him, he was beaten beyond recognition and then was ultimately crucified. The most astonishing thing happened afterward, even though the tomb where Jesus' body was laid was guarded by soldiers. On the third day, it was reported that Jesus had risen from the dead. There were accounts of Jesus' followers seeing him, as well as several hundred people confirming an encounter with him. The high priests don't want to talk about it, they tell everyone that the body was stolen.

While seated at the gate, Ariel had hours to ponder the man called Jesus of Nazareth and the reactions of the religious leaders and the followers of Jesus. It helped to fill his time at the gate asking for alms, yet he still did not know what to think of Jesus. Ariel knew that the religious leaders did not want Jesus or his followers to have any more influence in the area. Ariel thought that the true impact of Jesus would be seen if the disciples of Jesus remained faithful and strong in the ministry or if they faded away as others have in the past.

Ariel never imagined that he would be anywhere else, or do anything else, other than beg at the gate. He got up each morning, got ready, and was carried to the gate. At sundown, he was picked up and returned home, to repeat the next day. This was his life and his future.

The Gate Beautiful faced east, receiving the bright rays. For most of the morning hours, Ariel sat in the full sun. When it was cool, it warmed him, but today the weather was warm and the sun's heat beat down on him. As the morning faded into the afternoon, Ariel was relieved that the shadow of the wall was beginning to provide a little shade, which was a relief.

The shadows grew in length, indicating that the hour of prayer was at hand. Ariel observed the men and women begin to arrive for prayer. The shops and businesses closed for the day allowing them to come to prayer. Soon, the arrival of people passing through the gate stirred all the beggars to try to draw the people to give before entering the temple.

The voices of the beggars began crying out to them, saying, "Have mercy, sir," or "Alms for the poor," or "Just a mite will help," and other ways of asking for alms. Ariel's voice joined that of the rest of the beggars. The sound of coins landing in the cups of the beggars could be heard; this was the prime time for receiving alms.

Ariel had learned over the years to try to make eye contact with people and then ask for alms. It is harder to ignore him when they look at him and see the need. As the hour drew closer for prayer, more people were hurrying toward the gate. Ariel noticed two men who were looking his way. He continued to look at them to make eye contact with them.

"Have mercy on me," Ariel said when he knew they were looking at him.

Both men looked at him. Ariel sensed something different as he looked at the two men.

Ariel was startled when one of the men said, "Look at us." Ariel looked back at the men, hoping that their attention to him would result in getting something from them.

Ariel, staring at the men, heard the first man say, "Silver or gold, I do not have, but what I have, I give to you. In the name of Jesus Christ of Nazareth, walk!"

Ariel was shocked by his words. Before he could react, the man grabbed his right hand to help him up. He felt a sensation of power in his ankles and feet. Immediately, he was on his feet and walking. Without a thought, he went with the two men into the temple. He had forgotten the cup of alms that he had collected. Overcome with the excitement of his miraculous healing, Ariel was jumping, walking, and praising God. It was as if there was a fountain of praise bubbling out of him. He wanted to be in the temple to praise God.

Ariel was laughing and crying, then he would jump and spin around, and he would begin to shout and weep as he praised God for his mercy. His elation was contagious to the others within the courts of the temple. People began to observe him. At first they watched him, then the realization of who he was became evident to the onlookers.

When a few men who frequently gave Ariel alms drew close to confirm his identity, they questioned him, "Are you the beggar that sits at the Gate Beautiful?"

Ariel did his best to answer the men, between jumping and praising God, saying "Yes, I am that man."

More people realized that he was the beggar from the Gate Beautiful. The wonder and amazement of his healing drew more people to him. Unable to contain his gratitude to the Lord, he told his story to anyone who drew near to him. Ariel was told that the men who healed him were Peter and John, followers of Jesus.

Ariel knew that he had to know more about Jesus. The instantaneous strength that went to his feet and ankles had to be from God. Then an incredible desire to worship God would come over him again.

Ariel saw when Laban and Nathaniel came into the temple. They were carrying the seat that had been used for so many years to take him home. Ariel's brothers looked confused and were searching the crowd. Ariel was gone from his spot at the gate. They wondered if something had happened to him.

Ariel was excited to see them. His face held a huge smile and the joy within him overflowed again. He ran over to his brothers, jumping and hugging them, saying "Isn't this wonderful!"

He grabbed Nathaniel's robe, then turned to Laban saying, "I know it is a miracle! It was Peter and John, followers of Jesus of Nazareth. They healed me. Look at my feet, they are not turned in any longer! I am standing. I have even been running! There is no weakness in them. Praise God Almighty!"

Stunned by what they saw, Nathaniel and Laban couldn't speak. They just looked at him in disbelief. Laban looked around the temple. He placed his hands on his hips and stared at Ariel.

Nathaniel stood with a glazed look as he leaned on the pole of the traveling seat. How could it be that this morning his feet were limp and turned inward? He had never stood on his own or even taken a step. Now his feet are no longer turning in, and he is walking, jumping, and spinning around. It was the men who followed Jesus of Nazareth who did this?

Ariel answered excitedly, "Yes, yes, Amazing isn't it?"

Laban asked Ariel, "How did this happen? I don't understand."

Nathaniel bent over and touched his feet and ankles, then shook his head.

Ariel said to them, "I was in my normal place at the gate when they saw me asking for alms. The men, Peter and John, that follow Jesus of Nazareth said to me, 'Silver or gold, I do not have, but what I have, I give to you. In the name of Jesus Christ of Nazareth, walk.'

"Then Peter grabbed my hand and pulled me up, I felt a sensation of power in my ankles and feet. I was standing and then I started walking. I haven't stopped walking, jumping, or running since.

"My brothers, look, I can walk! Do you realize? I'm not lame and I'm not a beggar anymore! I have been healed! I will never have to come to the temple to beg! Nathaniel and Laban, you will never have to carry me to and from the temple ever again!"

Ariel added, "If Jesus of Nazareth can do this, what more is he able to do? I want to know. Come, let us worship God and learn more of Jesus of Nazareth."

His brothers still stunned walked with Ariel toward Peter, John and other followers of Jesus of Nazareth. As they neared the group, Ariel could hear Peter and John reminding the leaders, that it was by their hands, that Jesus Christ of Nazareth was arrested, beaten, and crucified. Peter then told the crowd that God raised Jesus from the dead.

Peter then turned to Ariel and said, "See this man, he was crippled. Now he is whole. It was the power of Jesus of Nazareth that healed him and he is able to stand before you."

The silence in the temple was palpable. Peter continued speaking with authority in his voice as he told them Jesus is the only one who can save; there is no other way to be saved. We must be saved through him.

At that statement, a priest stood telling everyone to leave the area so that they could speak amongst themselves. When alone they began to discuss Ariel's miracle and Peter and John.

Many of the men commented and marveled that these men were not educated. But it was evident that Peter and John had been with Jesus and that they had a boldness to speak.

The leadership discussed how people in the temple were going to Ariel and rejoiced with him over his incredible healing.

They realized that the presence of Ariel in the temple and that he was standing with Peter and John made it difficult to deny the miracle. Everyone in Jerusalem knew that Ariel had been the beggar at the gate for forty years.

The temple council commanded Peter and John not to speak or teach in the name of Jesus.

Peter and John were not phased by their threat. Peter's response silenced the council. He told them that it is more important to do what is right in the sight of God than in the sight of man.

The crowd from the temple began to thin as people made their way home. The miracle of Ariel was on the lips of witnesses as they took the news with them.

The afternoon sun began to cast a colorful orange hue over the temple, Peter and John were still at the temple when Ariel started to walk toward home. Ariel looked down at his feet and he felt a wave of astonishment. He was walking with his brothers, Nathaniel and Laban on the streets that he had traveled for so many years. Today, though, he set his foot on the streets for the very first time.

Stopping in the middle of the street, Ariel spoke to his brothers and said, "This morning you carried me to the temple; my feet were turned in and limp. I had never stood, never taken a step. Now I walk beside you! It wasn't until Peter and John told me to stand in the name of Jesus Christ of Nazareth. My brothers, I choose this day to be a follower of Jesus of Nazareth!"

Ariel told his brothers, "I must find Peter and John and the rest of those that follow Jesus."

Nathaniel and Laban watched as Ariel turned, shouted praises to God Almighty, and ran down the street to return to the temple to join Peter and John.

Chapter 4

OUT OF THE TOMBS

And they came over unto the other side of the sea,

into the country of the Gadarenes.

And when he was come out of the ship,

immediately there met him out of the tombs

a man with an unclean spirit.

Mark 5:1-2 KJV

The weather had turned cold along the Sea of Galilee. Abigail was aware that the nights had been even colder. She sighed deeply as she pulled on her heavy robe. She couldn't help wondering about her son, Javan. He was always in her thoughts. Walking over to the small oven, she added a few sticks to bake the bread and warm the room.

A gust of chilly air came in with Seth as he entered the room from outside. He moved closer to the oven, rubbing his hands together and savoring the heat it was starting to produce. Seth noticed his wife standing at the window, holding the covering back and looking out. He noticed that her eyes were full of tears. He knew the tears were the worry that was in her heart.

He saw it nearly every day. He reached out to her, pulled her in closer and said, "Do you want to take food to him?"

Abigail replied, through her muffled sobs, "Yes, and a blanket."

Seth said softly "Let's eat, then we will take him some bread and a blanket."

Javan was Abigail and Seth's only child. Seth was so excited when Abigail was with child. They had waited for so long for him. Javan was robust and lively. Seth was so proud of him. The child learned to walk and talk quickly, and schooling also came easily. He was a likable boy who made friends effortlessly. He would often help the elderly neighbors carry water from the well or tend to some of their other needs.

The little family went to the synagogue regularly and did their best to live their faith. Javan completed all the classes and requirements of the Jewish faith. Seth and Abigail wanted the best for him. They provided him with education and training from prominent teachers. Javan worked in his father's business from an early age. He proved to be talented in business too. It appeared as though anything he put his hand to, he excelled at it.

After a while, Javan became restless working with his father. One day he told his father he wanted his own business. Seth understood Javan's desire to have his own business. When Javan came of age, he decided to join a group that traveled selling their goods throughout the region. Soon Javan left with the group as a vendor selling beautiful rugs and tapestries.

Abigail and Seth prayed for him when he set out with the traveling troop.

They would listen intently to Javan's stories on his first few visits home. He excitedly told them what he had seen in the different cities and places where he had traveled. Over time, Seth began to observe subtle changes in Javan that concerned him.

After a year passed, Javan's visits home became less frequent. Then on one visit, Abigail noticed that Javan was wearing a necklace with a talisman charm. When she asked him about it, he simply answered that it was a gift given to him by one of the vendors in his group. She questioned why he was wearing it because a talisman was not a godly symbol. Javan quickly told her not to worry about it, saying he wore it to bring success to his business.

"As a Jew, our trust is not with anything or anyone other than God Almighty," Abigail reminded him.

Javan chuckled at his mother. But when she began again to caution him, he held up his hand and said dryly, "Mother, there is a big world out beyond this little city. Some things can help to obtain money, favor and other things from people."

Abigail listened to his response, but it distressed her. "Do you think that necklace honors God?" she asked.

Javan, feeling challenged by her questions, answered defensively, "Mother, my business has grown since I started wearing this necklace. Now you want me to take it off, because of some rules set by people long ago. It is my business and I will do what it takes for success."

The conversation ended. Abigail felt the sting of his words and knew that she could not discuss it with Javan. Later, she told Seth about the necklace with the talisman and how Javan had reacted to her questioning it.

Seth told her that he would look for an opportunity to talk with him about it.

The rest of the visit was strained. Abigail tried to overcome the tension that she knew was between them. Abigail was surprised that Javan did go with them to prayer at the temple, but it was obvious that he went from duty, not from desire.

They became aware with each of Javan's visits that he was changing even more. He did not wear the prayer garment any longer. He would not join in the morning prayers with Abigail and Seth and he even declined to go to the temple. Several times Seth attempted to speak with Javan about the changes, but each conversation ended with Javan telling his father to let him make his own choices.

After the visit, Seth and Abigail dedicated more time at the temple to pray for their son. At first, when neighbors and friends would inquire about Javan, Seth and Abigail did not know what to say. They chose to answer them vaguely saying that he is enjoying the travel and seeing many new things.

Over the next few years there were fewer and fewer visits from Javan. Seth and Abigail knew Javan was was falling away from the Jewish faith. Their cautions did nothing to alter his opinion of the path he had chosen. They watched helplessly as Javan drifted further from his heritage, faith and from them. Even so, they were committed to daily offer prayer for him.

They had confidence that as they prayed God would give Javan opportunities to return to his faith. Seth and Abigail spoke often of the life of King David, saying that even though he sinned, he would come back to the Lord, confess his sin and be restored. They remembered that Sampson had returned to the Lord at the end of his life. Even though Jonah disobeyed the Lord and was swallowed by a great fish, he did repent. They also remembered Adam and Eve and the great price of their disobedience. God promised that he would send a Messiah, who would restore man's relationship with him. They would encourage each other with stories of their patriarchs and other people of their faith to remember that God loves and watches over his children. He doesn't give up on them.

There was one visit by Javan with Seth and Abigail that was a turning point. As soon as he arrived, it was as evident he was a different person. His kind and gentle nature was replaced with judgment and ridicule. Javan arrived on the morning of the Sabbath. Later, as evening approached, the table was being set for the Sabbath meal. Abigail invited Javan to come to the table. His reluctance was obvious even though he sat with them. But, when Abigail began the prayer of invitation for the presence of the Lord to come into the home, Javan immediately became agitated and irritated by the prayer. Soon after, as the meal proceeded, his agitation grew into anger. He startled his parents when he got up abruptly declaring all of this was outdated tradition. Javan left the table and went to his room. Early the next morning, he left without even saying goodbye. After that incident, a year passed before Javan returned home.

At that visit, his bad treatment of his parents intensified. He was arrogant, sarcastic, and hateful. He criticized them for their lifestyle. He told them that their beliefs were embarrassing. Why could they not understand it was nothing more than old fables passed from one generation to another? He then explained to them that he had been able to experience many ways to worship, even other gods. He told them that they needed to understand that Jehovah is not the only god to worship.

Seth was horrified by Javan's declaration. How could his son, who had lived in a devout Jewish home really believe those lies? He had practiced this faith sincerely. He had completed all the requirements of the Jewish faith. Now for him to renounce it all and embrace idolatry, they just could not understand.

Seth and Abigail continued faithful to pray for their son. They hoped that someone would be able to convince him that the path he was on was dangerous.

For the next several years, Javan did not visit at all. Seth and Abigail grew desperate to know how and where he was. They wondered if something had happened to him. They did not know if he was alive or dead. Unfortunately, they had no way to try to find him without knowing his travel route. They had to wait for news. Finally, the vendors that he traveled with arrived in town. Seth and Abigail were hopeful that they would see Javan. They went in search of him, but he was not there. Their concern intensified to find out what had happened to their son.

They inquired about Javan with each of the vendors. Finally, one man told them that Javan had left the traveling group a couple of years before and was living with a group that worshiped Baal.

Abigail gasped when she heard where Javan was. Seth walked slowly home with Abigail leaning on him. His heart was broken, he could not understand how Javan could have made such choices. As they walked, he could feel her pain as her body shook as she wept. While he walked with her, he wanted to take her pain and sorrow, but he could hardly carry his own. He tripped as he walked; his vision blurred by the tears in his eyes. He had entered a new level of despair for Javan.

The friends of Seth and Abigail could see the effect all this was having on them. Seth's face seldom held a smile; he immersed himself in his work, spending long hours in his shop. Abigail's hair turned gray, and her face only showed sadness. There was no sparkle in her eyes as before. Their evenings were filled with silence. They knew each other's burdens. They talked through the situation many times over. There were no more words to be said to each other about Javan. Their only relief of their sorrow was to surrender it to God Almighty, again and again.

Seth and Abigail made daily trips to the temple to pray. Once, when Seth was very distraught, he went to the temple alone and sat along the wall in the court and wept. A gentle old Rabbi moved closer and then lowered himself to sit beside him.

"Seth, I know the burden is heavy, tell me as if you were telling Our Father Almighty," the Rabbi said with compassion.

He told the Rabbi the story of their son and his decisions over the years and the toll it had taken on his wife as well. The old Rabbi listened to the broken heart of the father regarding his son who now is far from home and his faith. Seth told the Rabbi he was also trying to support his wife, as she worries for her son, too. Seth poured everything out, his voice growing hoarse with emotion. With his eyes red and swollen from weeping and his face still furrowed with worry, Seth asked the Rabbi, "What did I do wrong?"

The Rabbi took a deep breath, and put his hand on his shoulder and said, "Seth each person must choose for themselves." He continued saying, "Parents teach and instruct their children about faith and how to do the right thing. Then there comes a point where the child accepts or rejects believing in God Almighty for themselves.

"Seth, now is not the time to give up praying for him. We have no idea how God is using your prayers. We must hold on to the confidence that God is at work in your son's life. He is giving Javan every opportunity to come back to Him. Didn't the prophet Isaiah say, 'Surely the arm of the Lord is not too short to save, nor his ear too dull to hear.'"

The Rabbi assured him that he would be praying, as well, for Javan to return to his faith in Jehovah God.

Seth returned home knowing that God had brought them the Rabbi, as a friend. He didn't feel so alone. He was glad that he had gone to the temple, his heart was more at peace. For the next months, Seth and Abigail found some days were easier to carry the worry and burden. But, every day they asked God to touch Javan's heart. As they prayed for him, they were comforted in knowing that God knew exactly where Javan was.

It was a bright summer's day when there was a knock at their door. Seth opened the door to see three men. Two of the men were clean and neatly dressed; however, the third man with them looked unkept and skittish, his eyes were empty and lost.

As Abigail came to the door, shortly after Seth, she heard him gasp and then she saw the look of distress on Seth's face. She saw Seth staring at the third man and she followed his gaze. It was as if she had been hit in the stomach. Her hands went over her mouth as she tried to take a breath. Her legs felt weak, she was not sure they would hold her up.

This shell of a man who stood before them was her son, Javan. Seth was staring at Javan, his eyes now full of sorrow as he listened to one of the men tell him that Javan had been living in their community, but recently he had been having some health problems. The men did not say much more to Seth; their only comment was that Javan had asked the men to take him home to Gerasenes. The men soon left without giving any more information.

Abigail drew close to Javan, searching his face and eyes of the boy she loved so much. Through her shattered heart said, "We're glad you have come home, Javan."

Javan stared at her as she spoke. His eyes lost the look of confusion for a moment, and he seemed relieved to see his parents. But, at once his face became twisted and his eyes filled with fear.

Seth and Abigail were grateful that he was home and they would do whatever was needed for his recovery. They had asked God to bring him home, and he did. They rejoiced even though they knew that Javan was deeply troubled.

As Seth quickly examined Javan's outward condition, his hands were shaking, his eyes were darting around the room and he looked like he was ready to run. The man that stood before him was filthy, in clothing that was dirty and torn and whose hair was matted. He was mumbling to himself and made erratic movements with his hands. It was when Seth looked into the eyes of his son that he felt an anguish that gripped his very being. The eyes told him that Javan was trapped inside.

Seth knew that even though Javan was home, there was a long road ahead for his healing and recuperation. Seth began to walk toward a room and then told Javan to follow. Javan shuffled, hardly picking up his feet, as he followed his father. They entered the room where he could wash and change his clothing.

Javan just stood there; it was as if he did not know what to do. Seth told him to remove his clothing to wash. He did not react or respond. It seemed like Javan didn't understand what his father was telling him. Seth began to comprehend the damage and the depth of Javan's condition.

Seth gently moved him over toward the bathing tub. Then as he helped Javan off with his tunic, he grimaced as he saw slash marks on his arms, legs and abdomen. Some of the slashes were open and festering; others looked older and were healed. Seth struggled to hold in the horror of the slashes. He wondered how Javan had come to have these wounds.

Seth filled the tub with water for Javan to bathe in, and he washed his son like he used to when he was a little boy. He spoke softly to him as he washed his hair and face, then scrubbed his back. Seth gently washed and examined his arms and legs which were full of cuts. He carefully had Javan stand to dry him off. He put salve on the cuts that were open and bandaged his arms and legs. It required all of Seth's strength not to weep as he saw the condition of his son's body.

Javan was so very thin, and his skin was a sallow color. His eyes were empty, and there was no emotion on his face. When Seth combed his son's hair, he looked at his face and he wished for the little boy of long ago, before all of this happened. Seth took a deep breath to muster his courage and quiet his aching heart.

Once clean and dressed, Seth led Javan to the table to eat, he could see Javan's eyes shifting from side to side as if he were listening to sounds on either side of him.

Abigail came in carrying warm bread, broth and cheese, and then she said in her most cheerful voice, "Javan, we are so glad you..." Before she was able to get the rest of her sentence out, he had grabbed the food from her and was shoveling it into his mouth. He held the food that fell to the table until he could eat it.

Abigail tried not to scream, but the shock surprised her it just escaped. She looked over to Seth. Her heart was pounding. She did not know what to do.

Seth looked at his son and said with his full voice, "Javan! Sit down!"

Javan looked around the room and then at his parents. He stared at them for a moment, then he sat down.

Seth told him, "We have enough food, Javan."

Seth then calmly asked Abigail, "Do you have more cheese you can bring in?"

Abigail, fighting tears, left the room to get more cheese.

"Javan, do you know where you are?" Seth asked.

Javan looked at his father, then answered in a soft voice, "Yes, home."

His father asked, "We have enough food for you to eat your fill, do you need anything?"

Javan answered saying, "Food, hungry."

The way that Javan answered took Seth's breath away.

For Seth and Abigail, the next few days went from hard to horrible. At first, Seth tried to treat Javan like before, but he soon realized that was impossible. Abigail was afraid of Javan, since the scene at the first meal. Javan's language was limited and he had outbursts of shouting and aggression. Seth took him to doctors thinking he might have been hurt or fallen. They sought several doctors who would examine him, only for them to say that he was a lunatic and that nothing could be done.

They did not leave him at home alone, unsure of what he would do. At times he would make lots of noise and become very unruly. His outburst seemed more frequent in the morning and at night. When it was the Sabbath, he was agitated from sundown until sunrise.

Several weeks passed, and Javan was better physically but his mental stability was worsening. Javan would not leave his room, he had broken everything in there. Seth took everything out of the room only leaving his sleeping mat. Often, he would sit in the corner and chant or mumble while he held on to the talisman that was on the necklace. Other times, he would scream and shout all through the night.

Seth and Abigail were at a loss as to what to do for him. One evening, when the chanting, shouting, and screaming were almost unbearable, the old Rabbi visited them. The Rabbi sat with them all through the night. Even though he did not say much to them, the Rabbi's prayers for them brought much comfort. Seth and Abigail were grateful for the old Rabbi. They did not feel alone as they faced this difficult ordeal.

The next months, for Seth and Abigail, were filled with daily struggles. Javan seemed more terrorized and tortured from within, and his outbursts of shouting became more aggressive. Neighbors often complained about Javan's disruptions in the night with his screams that continued until morning. Seth and Abigail could not find a way to control him other than locking him in a room, but that did nothing about the noise.

Because of the numerous complaints about Javan, there were visits from the Roman authorities, who warned Seth and Abigail that they would have to come and take their son away if they could not control him.

Seth could not bear the idea that Javan would be imprisoned, but he knew something was desperately wrong.

Seth could no longer work at his shop; he needed to stay home. He remained awake through the night with Javan trying to keep him calm so that he would not scream or pound on the walls. Abigail knew that her boy was somewhere inside of the wrecked man who was locked in the room of their home. She and Seth prayed asking God to do something.

Seth could hear the sounds of men outside the door of his home before he heard the sound of knocking. The past week had been the worst for them with Javan. He knew that it was Roman soldiers coming for him.

When he opened the door, Seth saw an officer with a group of soldiers. They had chains and shackles hanging over their shoulders. The officer read the order to him, but his words were drowned out by the shouting and screams of Javan. Then Abigail came and stood beside Seth. They had tried to control him and care for him, but they were exhausted and broken. They knew that they could not avoid this outcome, it was too much.

Seth told Abigail to go into the other room and not to come out. Seth guided the men to the room where Javan was locked. He opened the door, Javan was pacing, waving his arms, screaming, spitting, and then pounding on the wall. His eyes were wild-looking. Seth at first tried to calm Javan with his soft voice, but the presence of the soldiers agitated him even more.

The officer told Seth to step aside. Then the soldiers moved in quickly and cornered Javan.

Seth watched from the opposite side of the room as Javan thrashed, fought, screamed, kicked, and bit them. Finally, they were able to hold him to the floor as they shackled his legs together, and then his arms. The soldiers continued to wrestle with him for control. The soldiers picked Javan up from the floor, by his arms and legs. They had also gagged him to stop the screaming and biting.

Seth looked in disbelief and horror at the scene. How could this be his son? It was as if his son had become a wild animal. He felt his legs lose their strength, he could no longer stand. He slid down the wall and wept uncontrollably.

A few moments later, he felt a hand on his arm, he looked over to see the old Rabbi weeping with him as they prayed.

Seth heard the soldiers moving through the house taking Javan out, but he could not move. His grief, fatigue and helplessness had drained him of all his strength. Then it was quiet. He raised his head looking around as if he was listening to the silence. Seth stood slowly; a weariness swept over him.

The Rabbi, standing at his side, patted Seth's shoulder as he looked into his eyes, and said, "This is not for you both to carry on your own. Come to the temple we will pray together." He then left.

Seth went into their bedroom and saw his wife on the floor. Her face told of her heart's agony. Seth went to her, he lowered himself to the floor beside her, he took her in his arms, and they wept.

The next morning, Seth awoke to someone pounding on his door. He was stunned when he opened the door to see the same Roman officer from yesterday standing there with four men.

"Do you have him here?" the officer asked angrily.

Seth was confused at first by the question, then realized he that he was speaking of Javan.

"No, you took him in chains, yesterday, Seth answered sharply. What happened?"

The officer, now with a look of alarm, questioned him again, "Are you hiding him?"

Seth growing frustrated, asked again, "What happened? Why don't you have him?"

"He broke the chains and escaped," the officer said.

Seth shouted his questions, "He escaped? Broke the chains?

Abigail was now at the door trying to understand what was happening. She realized that Javan had escaped and no one knew where he was.

The officer tried to assure them they were searching for him. Then he turned and left, along with the other men.

Seth looked at Abigail, then told her, "Let's go to the temple."

Abigail nodded with quivering lips and brimming tears in her eyes. Then Seth's comforting arms embraced her, renewing her strength.

The rest of the morning was spent at the temple. As they returned home, their hearts clung to the peace from praying, understanding that the Almighty God watched over their son.

Several weeks passed with no word of Javan, Seth had inquired several times at the garrison about him but he was given no information. Abigail and Seth's days were filled with ebbs and flows between worry then trust.

The weeks became months with no information about Javan. Seth and Abigail began to have the conversation that perhaps something had happened to Javan.

There came a breakthrough one morning while Seth and Abigail were praying at the temple. The old Rabbi approached them sharing, "Someone has brought some news that I believe *could* be about Javan."

Seth stood behind Abigail, he put his hands on her shoulders, as they listened to the Rabbi.

"A fisherman came to the temple speaking of a man that is living among the tombs north of the city near the coast. He said that he screams for hours, cuts himself and that cannot be bound even with chains."

The old Rabbi watched the couple react to the news.

"I will go to see who this fisherman speaks of," Seth responds quickly.

"We will go," came the familiar voice of his wife, Abigail.

The couple walked the road out of town, toward the place of the tombs near the coast. Stopping from time to time to rest on boulders that were evidence of rockslides from the nearby cliffs. They breathed in the salty fragrance of the sea; it had been so long since they had come to the sea or anywhere else. They continued walking toward the tombs as apprehension filled their hearts.

Would they be relieved to know he was there, or dread that he lived there in the tombs in the open elements of wind and cold?

A piercing scream filled the air and their hearts. They identified that scream. Javan was there.

They looked around to try to follow the sound of the screams to locate where he was in the tombs. After searching the area, Seth found him standing on a grave. He pointed to show Abigail where he was. Javan was holding rocks in his hands. His body was nearly covered in cuts, dried blood, and filth. Hanging from his wrists were shackles with links of chains. He screamed while he looked all around. He then scraped his chest with the rock and crouched down like a beaten dog.

The scene of her son's torment overwhelmed Abigail. She turned, putting her face into Seth's chest. Seth knew they had found their son and they had seen what they needed to.

They returned home as the sun was setting and Seth took his wife directly to their room. She silently readied for bed. He placed the blankets over her and then prayed asking the Lord God to rescue their son.

Since finding Javan, Seth made the trip to the tombs at least once a week. He would leave food, and from time to time a blanket or clothing. At first, when he went, Seth tried to get his attention, but it seemed that Javan could not hear anything other than what was in his head. Abigail would go with him when she felt up to it. Each trip to the tombs drained her energy and emotions, it would require days to recover.

When Seth walked home, he agonized over seeing Javan. His thoughts would be a mixture of prayer and seeing the reality of the situation. Was this Javan's life now? Is there anything that could help him? How can anyone be restored from where Javan is at? In the midst of this, his greatest fear was that he would find him dead because he had succumbed to the weather or something else.

For the past six months, the old Rabbi prayed and talked with Seth, and told him about a man from the Nazareth area who had done miracles. He had healed a blind man and preached unlike anything he had ever heard. Even though Seth listened to the Rabbi, he was not interested in any traveling preachers.

If Seth were honest with himself, there were times that he would struggle not to give up on praying for Javan. It had been more than five years since Javan last came home. The other day he told God he did not have any more words to pray. Since then when he would go to the temple he would just sit in silence.

People within the community often spoke about the man in the tombs. To some, he was the subject of jokes and ridicule. For others, he was to be feared, while others would go and watch his unusual behavior. Few were aware that the man in the tombs was Seth and Abigail's son.

For some, it has almost become a sport for people to try to bind him with straps and chains to get him out of the tombs, but nothing could hold him. Those who have tried to catch and bind him realized instantly that his strength was uncommon. They were so terrified after their encounter that no one has attempted to restrain him more than once.

One morning seemed brighter to Abigail when she looked out the window as she did every morning. A few birds were singing nearby putting a melody in her heart. Seth entered the room and then heard Abigail humming. She had not sung or hummed for so long.

Seth asked her if she noticed the birds singing outside. Abigail smiled and told him that the bird's song had put a song in her heart. She stirred the fruited water and then put the bread on the table.

Abigail told Seth, "I want to go to the temple to pray today."

"You haven't gone in days, is there something special?" he asked confused.

"I have the desire to go and pray," she said, while giving him a plate of fruit.

Seth noticed that she didn't have the worn drawn look on her face. They walked the familiar streets toward the temple. Several of the neighbors greeted them as they passed by.

It was about noon as they entered the temple. Abigail scanned the court to look for the old Rabbi. Seth knew that Abigail was acting differently, but he was unsure what to think.

Seth felt his spirit lift as he entered the court; he sensed lightness and a desire to pray. His eyes searched for and found Abigail in the court. She was talking with the old Rabbi. Seth joined them and then mentioned that he sensed something different while he stood in the court.

The old Rabbi said to them, "Now it is time to pray. The Lord has put a new hope within you."

The Rabbi said he perceived that God was moving.

Abigail commented that for the first time in years she didn't have the sense of worry and dread that had become common to her.

Seth was surprised by her statement, but agreed that he didn't feel a heaviness of fear about what was happening with Javan.

That afternoon, they left the temple with a calm they had not enjoyed for years.

As they walked through a busy marketplace toward home, they heard a commotion. Some men had come into town yelling about pigs running off a cliff and drowning. Seth and Abigail stopped and listened to the ranting of the men, trying to understand what they were talking about.

One man was shouting to the many people that were there, "The man from Nazareth, it is his fault all my pigs are gone, two thousand, not a one left!"

Then the herdsman urged the crowd, "Who will go with us so that we may plead with this man to leave, he can't stay here. He destroyed my herd!"

Seth and Abigail listened to the men as they ranted, It seemed that they were successful in gathering a group of men to return to urge the man from Nazareth to leave.

Seth and Abigail decided to go home and not concern themselves about pigs.

The sun had just fallen beyond the horizon, taking with it the warmth of the day, when the couple reached home. They were settling at the table enjoying remnants of the fire and the calm of the evening. Seth was watching Abigail repair the pocket in a robe when there was a knock at the door. Seth looked at Abigail with a questioning look, then walked to the door. They were not accustomed to visitors in the daytime, rarely in the evening or night.

Seth opened the door enough to see who was there. He saw a man standing with a smile on his face and cautiously asked him, "Can I help you?"

"Father," Javan said with a smile.

When Seth stared at a man who resembled Javan, his heart started to beat hard. He stood silently scrutinizing the man at the door. He cautiously allowed his mind to hope. His thoughts began to spin.

"Didn't I pray for my son to come home? Didn't I ask for God to rescue him?" Seth questioned himself.

"Javan, is that you?" Seth asked, breaking the silence and displaying his uncertainty.

"Yes!" Javan replied.

Seth let the door swing open. He blinked his eyes, wondering if this was real. He stared at this man who was calm, clean, and dressed. Seth was trying to grasp the scene before him, looking into his eyes. Yes it was Javan!

Abigail came to the door wondering what was happening. She put her hands over her mouth to quiet the shout of praise to God. She hugged Javan, as she continued to cry and praise God.

Finally, Seth motioned for him to come into the house. Then he reached out grasping Javan's shoulders and tried to absorb that his son was actually standing in front of him. At that moment, it was as if a dam had broken within Seth. He pulled Javan tight against him. Several times Seth pulled back from Javan to look at him and then quickly embrace him again. At first, Seth was silent but the tears of joy spoke for him.

Even though Abigail was excited that Javan was home, she was cautious of Javan's condition. She watched as her husband and son embraced. She walked around the men as they embraced to better assess his health and condition.

Javan then turned to his mother. She reached up to stroke his hair. Then she cupped his face in her hands. Abigail stared deeply into Javan's eyes, and said, "My boy, you are home!"

They smiled as they stared at each other. The smile captured the thankfulness and love they had for each other. Javan picked her up and he spun around with her as they hugged. When he put her down, she took his hands in hers then lifted them to her lips and kissed them. She often had to wipe the flow of joy in the form of tears from her face.

Javan took the hands of his mother and kissed them. He gathered her in his arms again. Then he kissed the top of her head.

Javan, thick with emotion, said, "Yes, mamma, I am home."

She felt the warmth of his embrace, her eyes closed as she imprinted this memory in her heart. As he held her, she thought: if this is a dream, don't ever wake me.

The three of them were lost in the bliss of Javan's return. They were unaware of time, it didn't matter, Javan was home. No words were spoken or needed, as the embraces, pats of affection, kisses, looks of love and tears of joy expressed the depth of the emotion of their hearts.

When Abigail finally let go of Javan, with a smile that seemed to fill the room, she said to him, "Sit at the table, let me get you something to eat."

Javan put his arm on his father's shoulder as they moved to the table. They took their usual places. It was as if Javan had never left.

"Son, what happened?" Seth, sitting with his hands clasped and head bowed, asked with a tremble in his voice.

"Oh, Father, it was the man from Nazareth, his name is Jesus," Javan said. "Have you heard of him?"

Seth answered, "A Rabbi spoke to me of him recently, but I know little."

Abigail neared the table with a pitcher and a plate, when there was a soft knock on the door.

Surprised, Seth looked at Abigail and Javan, then moved toward the door, which he opened just a sliver and peered out. Before he could ask who was there, he heard the voice of his friend —Rabbi Amos.

The Rabbi said in a low voice, "I know the hour is late, my friend, however, I might have some good news for you."

Opening the door, Seth smiled at his friend. The Rabbi had quietly been a strength for them through the years of this devastating ordeal. He was so grateful for this man, it was fitting that God had brought him in this moment.

"Please come in my dear friend, we have some great news too," Seth said.

Seth motioned for him to follow him. When the Rabbi rounded the corner and beheld Javan sitting with Abigail at the table with smiles that nearly hid their eyes, he let out a shout of praise and threw his arms into the air. He turned in circles in excitement, clapping his hands and even singing the words of a song.

Looking upward he cried, "You, oh God, are faithful. When we see it or not, you are faithful. Each day your goodness and mercy are on display to your children. You heard our prayers from the temple and the prayers deep within our hearts."

As Javan watched his mother, father, and the Rabbi, he knew they had been praying for him. Javan felt a love and peace sweep over him afresh.

Soon Seth, Abigail, and Javan had joined the Rabbi in worshiping Jehovah, God Almighty. Their excitement and gratitude poured out of them. They knew it was God who had brought Javan home.

After a time, Abigail asked the Rabbi to sit with them to hear how God had worked.

The Rabbi thanked them as they sat at the table. Abigail brought cups of fruit water for everyone. Javan was too excited to eat the bread and cheese his mother had brought him.

Seth said, "Rabbi, Javan arrived home not long before you arrived. Javan was about to tell us what had happened that brought him home. We are anxious to hear the miracle that we see in our son."

Javan looked to his parents and then to the Rabbi. He took a drink of the fruited water. Breathing deeply he began his story.

"It is still amazing that I am sitting here at home with you. Just a few hours ago I was trapped and hopeless."

His smile faded as he searched for words to start. The sorrow in his was voice evident when he began to tell them, "There are no words to describe the horrible torment that I had been in. I had no thoughts of my own. I constantly heard voices telling me that I was forever trapped. I did not want to cut myself; it was if I had to. I would do things that I did not want to do, I could not stop myself.

"When people would try to tie me up or bind me in chains, something inside would take over. I would feel a strength that I knew was not mine. It was a strength so strong that I could snap the chains and shackles. The constant blasphemy and profanity in my mind drowned out my ability to think or reason. I was trapped. I knew that evil was within me. Yet I had no power to tell it to go, overcome it, or escape it."

Javan sat calmly, with his hands folded on the table.

"Until this morning." he said.

Javan's smile returned, and he turned his gaze to his parents and his eyes glistened moist with tears.

"This morning when a boat arrived at the shore, I knew something was different. I watched as the boat approached the beach not far from the tombs. When the man stepped out of the boat, I could sense a holy authority within him."

Javan stopped speaking. He began to sob, overcome with emotion.

"I knew, he was there for me." Javan said in just a whisper.""Suddenly, I had an overwhelming desperation to get to him. I have never felt so determined. It did not matter if I had to fight everything within me. I had to get to him. At first, my feet would not move. But when I looked at Jesus, I could sense the power to move my feet and legs. I recognized at that moment, that this was my chance. I began to walk stiffly with each step, but there were things inside of me that were trying to stop me.

"As I continued to focus on Jesus it became easier, and soon I was nearly running toward him. The whole time I was trying to get to Jesus, I was battling the blaspheming voices that said vile things against God and Jesus. They tried to tell me it was too late for me, that I belonged to them, and they had control over me and they would never let me go.

"The closer I got to Jesus, the louder the screaming was in my mind. I forced myself to keep my eyes on Jesus and I kept moving toward him."

Javan stopped for a moment to calm his emotions.

"I had to keep my eyes on Jesus to be able to move. I made my way through the tombs and then onto the beach where Jesus stood. He was waiting for me! As I came near, I fell on my knees in front of him.

" I was aware of the holiness and power in him. I somehow knew that Jesus could help me. I wanted him to understand I wanted to be free.

"Before I could speak a word, what was inside of me took over. It said to Jesus, 'What do you want with me? Jesus, Son of the Most High God. In God's name do not torture me.'

"Then Jesus spoke directly to what was in me," Javan said. "He told it to come out of me, and he called it an impure spirit. There was honor and authority in Jesus' voice. Immediately, I could feel the battle raging in my mind and body. Jesus was not intimidated at all by what was in me.

"Jesus asked, 'What is your name?'

"The evil within answered, 'My name is Legion, for we are many.'"

Javan stopped speaking and looked down at his hands. He took a deep breath and blew it out slowly. He raised his head and studied the faces of his parents and the Rabbi.

"The next part of what I am going to share might seem unreal, but let me assure you, it was very real." Javan began anew recounting his story, his voice was shaky and he hesitated often as he spoke, "What was inside of me was evil, and it spoke to Jesus. Legion begged Jesus over and over not to send him out of the area. On the hillside nearby there was a large herd of pigs. The demons began begging Jesus to send them into the pigs. Jesus permitted them, and all impure spirits came out of me and went into the pigs. Immediately all the pigs ran over a cliff and drowned."

Javan blew all the air out of his lungs. His eyes were closed. He opened them and said with a tearful smile, "That was the moment

I was free. I knew it because the nonstop cursing against God had ceased.

"I realized that I was naked and filthy. Some of the men with Jesus helped me wash and gave me clothing. After Jesus sent Legion to the pigs, the peace that came into me that was nothing like I have ever experienced. It was so wonderful. I still feel it, there is power in Jesus' peace.

"I don't feel dirty inside anymore."

Seth, Abigail and the Rabbi sat in stunned amazement.

Javan rubbed his hands together, then continue his miraculous story.

"After I washed and dressed, Jesus sat with me, and we talked. The sounds of a mob came toward where Jesus and I were seated. We noticed the herdsman leading them. Some were yelling about the pigs that had been lost. Others were shouting that the man who had sent the pigs over the cliff had to leave. Abruptly everyone stopped and went silent. They had caught sight of me, the man in the tombs, the one who cut himself and was able to break chains or shackles that were used to capture him. They saw me sitting calmly with Jesus. I was dressed, clean and in my right mind. Instantly the people became afraid. Ripples of comments could be heard through the crowd.

The people were shocked. Many were questioning what had happened. What power did this visitor have that could have this effect on the man in the tombs? The herdsman and others demanded Jesus to leave now."

Without warning Javan stood and began to pace the room. Seth, Abigail, and Rabbi Amos jumped in surprise.

After a moment, Javan began again, "Jesus and his followers gathered their things. Then returned to their boat. As Jesus began to enter it, I rushed to him. I pleaded with Jesus to take me with him. I didn't want to be away from him. I did not want to stay here. I wanted to go where no one knew me."

"Jesus told me that I could not go. Again, I begged him to let me stay with him, but Jesus told me to go home to my people and tell them how much the Lord has done for me, and how he has had mercy on me."

Javan stopped again, he breathed slowly for a moment.

Seth spoke softly to Javan, "Do you want to rest for a little while?"

Javan shook his head.

"It is not that I need to rest, I am overwhelmed," he said. "Today happened because you never stopped praying. Today God sent Jesus to me. God sent me another opportunity."

Javan sat at the table again, took a drink, and then said, "I want to tell you what happened from the beginning.

"It started when I noticed some of the men of the vendor's group were very wealthy. That is why I wanted to join the group; I wanted to have money. While I was with the group, I sold very little, everyone else was selling more. I couldn't understand why I wasn't selling. I had good quality items and the price was good. One day, I went to one of the successful men in the group. He gave me the talisman that you saw. He told me that it would attract wealth. The next few days, I sold more than ever, I was hooked.

"Soon I was making offerings at their altars, and even though I felt a warning in my heart, I wanted the money more. I did whatever they said to bring me wealth. Those choices took me to very dark places. They changed how I thought and how I saw people. If someone spoke to me about Jehovah or God Almighty, I began to have a physical reaction. Soon after, the thoughts against God started."

Javan commented sadly, "I knew that God used you to warn me, but I didn't listen to you. I think you both remember those days. I am so sorry.

"There were people in other cities where I was selling, who advised me to stay away from talismans, fortune tellers, mediums and other things that would take me away from Jehovah God. At first, I just ignored their advice, and then I rejected it completely. I ridiculed those people, telling them that they were narrow-minded and old-fashioned.

"With each choice I made, I gave up a piece of myself. I was falling deeper into the darkness and I didn't know how to get out."

Javan's eyes focused on the faces of his parents, then said, "But God kept coming after me because you never stopped praying."

Seth began to speak, at first haltingly as he was trying to control his emotions.

"My son, your mother, and I knew that our only way to help you was to pray. What else could we do? The battle was beyond our power and our strength. We had to constantly go to our God Almighty to pray and surrender you to Him, otherwise, the worry became too much."

Seth reached out to Abigail's hand as he continued, "My friend here, Rabbi Amos, has supported your mother and me for years. He has spent time praying for you too. He was here when the Roman soldiers took you away."

Javan responded, "I can not begin to tell you the power of those prayers. Initially, there were times I knew when you were praying, I would remember things from the Torah, I recalled the stories of Sampson and King David."

Abigail smiled through her emotion and said, "Those are the same stories we encouraged each other with."

"As time passed, every time you prayed, I felt the battle within me," Javan said. "Scriptures I had memorized long ago came to mind. Then the voices would tell me it was all a lie. The evil would tell me that I had gone too far, there was no forgiveness for me. Over the last few years, my mind has been filled with blaspheming against God. It told me I belonged to them and that I would never be free. They repeated day and night God didn't want me or love me because I had done too much. The evil one knew you were praying for me.

"Thank you for not stopping believing that God could rescue me. He sent Jesus to me today.

"Thank you," he repeated in a whisper.

Rabbi Amos cleared his throat as he looked at his hands then he gazed at Javan.

"Why do you think Jesus didn't let you go with him?"

Javan looked intently at the Rabbi, thought for a moment and then responded.

"Because, he told me to go home to my people. I am to tell everyone how much the Lord has done for me, and how he has had mercy on me."

Javan began to nod his head. It seemed to bring clarity to him as he contemplated his last statements.

"I am beginning to understand why Jesus would not allow me to go. My situation is well known all throughout the whole Decapolis area. News travels fast and I am sure that everyone in the region knows of my history, my encounter with Jesus and what happened to the pigs.

"I would have never believed that I would have ended up where I was. At first, it was little things, then another and another. Too quickly I was doing things that I can't even talk about. I want people to know that little steps away from Jehovah the Almighty God takes them into darkness. It is not all at once, but that is the destination.

"Even though that is where I was, who best could tell of the mercies of the Lord after I was set free from living in the tombs? I must tell the people of Jesus, his great mercy, and all that the Lord has done for me. People need to know that our faith in God is not an old fable, it is true!"

Javan's voice was strong and determined with his declaration.

Even though the night was silent, and the moon had moved across the night sky, a shout was heard from Rabbi Amos. Javan, Abigail, and Seth were startled and then they laughed.

"You got it, my boy!" the Rabbi said as he clapped his hands.

For another hour, they began to plan with Javan about his leaving to obey Jesus' command. The emotions of the night were beginning to show. When Abigail tried to hide a yawn, Seth suggested that everyone was drained and needed to rest.

Rabbi Amos agreed saying, "The enjoyment I received tonight is a highlight of my life. I have seen many things over the many years I have served my Lord. But nothing compares to seeing Javan at home, restored. My blessing was that Jehovah let me be a small part.

Javan commented to his father, "I feel like the Rabbi has a heart for Jehovah and has great faith, doesn't he?"

"Yes he does. He helped to keep the hope alive for us and urged us to continue in prayer," Seth said.

Abigail and Seth hugged Javan again as they went to their rooms. Even though they slept a little longer the next day, Javan was up first and was at the table praying. Later, Abigail and Seth came upon him at the table. They waited for a moment before they entered the room. They stood at the door listening to him share his heart with the Almighty God. This was not a dream. For years they had hoped for this day to come. Javan was home, healed and Jesus had set him free.

Javan told his parent as they ate, that he was going to go out to begin to do what Jesus had commanded. They went to the temple to pray and offer thanksgiving to the Lord before he left.

In the afternoon, Javan had set out to go to the cities in the region of Decapolis. He was to tell everyone of all the Lord has done and of his great mercies.

In the cities where he traveled many people had heard of the demoniac that lived in the tombs. He would begin by saying that he was that man. He told them of his choices and the consequences of them that took him there. When he shared that his parents never gave up praying for him, he always became emotional.

Often parents would tell Javen about their children. He was quick to tell them how the Lord had used the prayers of his parents.

At each encounter, he would begin to tell of the morning when a boat came to a beach near the tombs. A silence would always come over the crowd. Then, he would sense the same love and holy presence as he did the day that Jesus set him free. Javan described Jesus' authority over evil, and told his listeners that God does not want anyone in bondage. Each time, the people would be amazed by his story.

After he set out to follow Jesus' command, Javan remembered that moment when he was pleading to go with Jesus. Immediately he began to praise God and thanked him for sending him out to tell his story.

Javan, throughout his life, would remind people that he is no longer the man in the tombs because Jesus brought him out of the tombs to a new life.

Chapter 5

LOOK ONLY TO HIM

One day some parents brought their children

to Jesus so he could touch and bless them.

But the disciples scolded the parents for bothering him.

When Jesus saw what was happening,

he was angry with his disciples.

He said to them, "Let the children come to me.

Don't stop them! For the Kingdom of God

belongs to those who are like these children.

Mark 10:13-14 NLT

The market square was filled with cheery noises of the children giggling and calling out to one another as they ran through the streets. To some adults, as they watched and listened to the children's playful sounds, it brought a smile to their faces. They remembered their play times of long ago. Yet for others, who would listen to them, those sounds did not bring the same response. It was noise, it brought frustration, it interrupted their work and thoughts. They had long forgotten the enjoyment of childhood.

Today was like many other days, Leah walked through the streets of Jerusalem as she traveled from one job to the next. She stood for a moment, watching the activities of tradesmen, vendors, and the many people that filled the streets. When she saw the children running and playing and heard their laughter, she stopped and watched.

As she stood and listened to the children's carefree sounds, she did not realize that tears were streaming down her face. It wasn't until a woman stopped to ask her if she was all right.

Embarrassed, Leah excused herself and walked quickly to her next job to mend a rug. With each step she tried to compose herself.

For the past few years, Leah's life has been difficult. Her lifelong desire was to have a home and family, yet broken vows and lack of resources created many hardships for her and her children. Her family tried to help as much as possible, but with the heavy taxes due to Rome, and not having constant work, everyone was struggling to survive.

Leah did what she could; at times she washed clothing for others. She taught herself to mend rugs, tapestries, curtains and blankets to earn money. There was a time when she even gleaned the fields to feed her four children. Often, she felt tired, empty and lost. Even though, it seemed that each day grew harder than the last, Leah pressed on working to care for her children.

Lately, in nearly every home where Leah repaired the tapestries and rugs, the servants, guards, and the families spoke of Jesus of Nazareth. She learned from their conversations that Jesus, a Jew, had gathered a group of men to be his disciples. They traveled from town-to-town teaching about God in a very different way from what the Rabbis and Priests of the temple are teaching.

Then she heard of Jesus healing people. Some were rich, others were poor. Leah was intrigued that Jesus' ministry included all people, not just the Jews.

Since she began hearing of Jesus, she would listen for the latest news of where he had been and what he had done. Surprisingly, her mind was more occupied by Jesus and less on her troubles.

At the market, the well and even on the street, there were discussions every day of Jesus' activities. She had noticed, as she walked through the streets, the crowds were increasing because of Jesus. Those who had heard Jesus speak remarked how his teaching was so different. It was more personal. Others could not be silenced about what they had witnessed when Jesus healed people who were lame, blind and ill.

Leah repeatedly heard people say their lives were changed after an encounter with Jesus. She realized that everyone who had heard Jesus's teaching and observed his healings was drawn to know more. Many within the Jewish community have begun to attend his meetings, when he is in the area. Even some Romans have become curious about this man from Nazareth.

Recently, Jerusalem was buzzing with the news about Jesus going into the temple. He was angered when he saw the money changers and all the buying and selling of animals. He made a whip and drove out from the temple the sellers and their animals. He shouted to everyone that this was his father's house, not a house of merchandise.

She thought that Jesus had to have remarkable character and courage to react with so much authority in the temple. She began to remember the long-awaited promise that God would send a redeemer, the promised one. Could he be the promised one?

As time passed, when Leah went from house to house to work, everyone had an opinion about Jesus. But she thought of how he had driven out those who were making a profit to pray and to offer sacrifices. Leah had not gone to the temple for a long time, because of the high cost of the sacrifice.

She heard more news of Jesus healing many sick and that he had fed thousands with just a couple of fish and five loaves of bread. She wondered how he could have done such a feat. She wondered again, "Who was he? Is he a prophet, or the promised one?"

With every comment from a person who has seen or heard of Jesus' teaching, his message was that God sees us individually and that he cares for each of us. Leah felt a stirring within her weary heart, as she thought, "Does God see me?"

She silently wondered, "Does he see me when I am at home and look at my children and wish more for them than the life I had? Did he see that I didn't want them to have the drudgery of living as I do now. Life seems be so hard and with no hope?

"Did God hear me on the nights when despair would try to overtake me; when my heart would fight off the dark thoughts by calling out to you, God, for help. Did he hear me when I called for him to send someone or something that would make a difference in my life and the life of my children?"

As she considered all that Jesus was saying and doing in the area, it seemed as though she took a small step closer from wonder to belief that God sent this man.

One night, the weight of her burdened heart tried to convince her to give up. It was as though a blackness was sucking every bit of hope from within her. Instead of giving into the darkness and hopelessness, she chose to pour out her weariness and desperation by crying out to God.

"I believe this Jesus has been sent by you, God, and he is my answer, she said in prayer. "I believe you sent him to our people. Please help me, I need to know that you see our lives and our needs."

Immediately the darkness faded and the heaviness lifted. Leah felt peace come over her and her heart was relieved. She slept differently that night. When she awoke, she was refreshed. The weariness and hopelessness were gone.

That morning, Leah gathered her children and told them about all the things she had heard about Jesus of Nazareth. Leah told them of a well-known blind man from birth who, by Jesus' touch, was made to see again. She also shared about the leper who was healed, and how Jesus even touched him, though no one else would in fear of catching the leprosy.

Caleb, the oldest son, had mentioned that he had heard about Jesus from some of his friends who had told him that Jesus had healed a man at the pool of Bethsaida.

Ezra added that he wanted to go see what Jesus might do.

Priscilla and Sariah, her young daughters, told her that they were excited to go to the market with her.

Leah held the hands of Priscilla and Sariah tightly and told the boys to stay close to her as they walked down the chaotic streets of the market. They all were hoping to see Jesus.

Leah thought the best place to start would be to walk toward the street near the synagogue. That street was also crowded with vendors' carts, people going in every direction and dogs barking. They looked through the crowds of people at the synagogue for him, but he was not there. They continued to walk up and down so many streets. Priscilla and Sariah grew tired of walking and began to ask to go home.

Caleb went over to Sariah and Priscilla and asked them, "Did you know that mother has taken us on an adventure? We have to keep our eyes open to find Jesus."

"But I don't know what he looks like," Sariah answered.

"Let's see who can find him," Ezra asked with a smile.

"Oh, I think I will know what he looks like," Priscilla said to everyone.

"How will you know?" Leah asked.

"Momma, he will have love in his eyes, because if he heals people, that is love, right?" Priscilla said. Leah knew Priscilla would have something interesting like this to say.

Caleb laughed then said, "You are so right, Priscilla."

"Are we ready to start again?" Leah asked to her children.

Caleb took the Priscilla's hand, then they began to walk down the next street.

After turning a corner, a crowd of people had surrounded a man who was sitting on a rock. Leah felt power and peace as soon as she looked at him.

Just then, Priscilla came up to her and pulled down her hand saying, "Momma, can you see the love in his eyes? I think that is Jesus."

After observing the man on the rock, Caleb and Ezra came closer to their mother. They were all looking at each other, to see how each other reacted. Leah's heart was pounding as she recognized that this was Jesus, the one that she was looking for. Her thoughts held onto the desire that this would bring hope to her and her children.

They all stood watching Jesus and the people for several minutes. Caleb looked to Jesus and then his mother. Ezra looked to Jesus and then to Caleb. All the while, Leah couldn't take her eyes off of Jesus.

While she continued observing Jesus, she spotted Sariah and Priscilla walking toward Jesus by themselves. A follower of Jesus moved to stand in the path of the girls and motioned for them to move away from Jesus. Leah quickly stood to get to the girls. Before Leah had taken more than a step or two toward the girls, she heard Jesus tell the man to let the children come. Leah heard Jesus tell the people that the kingdom belongs to those who are like children. Then Jesus reached out his hand to Priscilla and Sariah inviting them to come.

Jesus smiled at Sariah, he cupped her face with both of his hands, looked into her eyes and smiled at her. Then he hugged her gently, Sariah smiled at him then moved aside and waited for Priscilla.

Jesus placed his hands on a boy's shoulders as he smiled at him. The boy nodded to Jesus, then ran off and began playing again. Leah watched Priscilla as she stood waiting for Jesus to see her.

Jesus then turned to Priscilla and reached out to her as she drew close. Priscilla spoke to him and pointed to Jesus' eyes. Jesus nodded and smiled at her and put his hands on Priscilla's head and then on her cheek. Priscilla hugged Jesus as if it was the most natural thing to do. She smiled at him, and walked back to where Sariah was waiting.

Sariah and Priscilla returned to her mother and the boys, while Jesus continued to bless other children.

"Yes, his eyes are full of love, he is a good man," Priscilla said. "Momma, it is like his eyes talk to your heart."

"Oh, when he held my face, it was like he was hugging me really tightly. I felt it down to my toes," Sariah added.

Leah wanted her boys to go over to Jesus, but the crowd was growing quickly. She knew that she couldn't push Caleb to go to Jesus. She chose to wait for a moment to see what would happen. Leah moved over to sit on some rocks and get a better view.

More children arrived and went up to Jesus as if they were drawn to him. Others were being taken over to him by a parent. Jesus touched each child tenderly and blessed them. It was obvious that he cared deeply for the children.

As Leah watched, she silently prayed that Caleb and Ezra would seek to touch Jesus.

Surprisingly, she saw that Jesus had a twinkle in his eyes and motioned to a young man, then he got up. The boy produced a ball from a pocket and threw it to Jesus. Jesus tossed it gently back.

Leah knew the ball toss game would attract the older children to Jesus.

When she finished her thought, she saw Jesus invite all the older children to get in a circle to play. Immediately Caleb and Ezra were in the circle. Jesus threw the ball to someone, and then they threw it back. No one knew where he would throw it next, everyone watched the ball, laughed, and enjoyed the game.

Caleb had the ball thrown to him. He studied the ball quickly; it was a stitched heavy muslin ball, filled with sand. Caleb thought he could make one as he threw it back. As he looked to Jesus to aim. He could feel a sense of peace as he focused on Jesus.

Ezra was anxious for his turn as he waited, he watched hoping that he would be next, but time after time it went to another. Just as Ezra was ready to give up, Jesus looked at him and threw the ball, and Ezra returned it with a smile. Unexpectedly, he felt a wave of love and peace. Now he understood what Priscilla and Sariah had told them.

The ball was tossed around and around to all those who were in the circle. Jesus looked at each one as the ball went back and forth between them.

Leah could sense love from Jesus as she observed her children and the rest of the people. She had forgotten the struggles, hardships and disappointments in her life. For the first time in a long time, she sensed joy and excitement for the future.

As midday came, the sun had grown hotter. Jesus stopped the game. Many children went up to him to thank him for playing.

While Leah watched, the followers of Jesus began to pick up their robes and packs, as Jesus wiped the perspiration from his face. To her surprise, she felt a little panic, he was leaving! She didn't want him to leave. When would she have another chance to experience this peace and love? She lowered her head to concentrate on the beautiful encounter with Jesus. She wanted to remember every moment of this time.

It was as if a whisper came in her ear and said, "Look to me." Her head raised looking to see who spoke to her. Then looked in the direction where Jesus was seated, and she realized that he was looking directly at her. As she focused on him, he nodded to her and then smiled. It was as if a dam broke within her. The years of hurt, fatigue, struggle and fear were washed away, and in its place were hope and peace.

She heard the whisper again, "Look only to me." With a full heart, she gazed at Jesus and nodded with a timid smile.

Jesus left with his men. They walked on the road out of Jerusalem. A crowd followed them as they left the area.

Leah and her children walked toward their tiny room that was home. Priscilla and Sariah chattered at first, but they began to struggle to keep up the pace.

"Do you want me to carry you for a little while?" Caleb asked Sariah. Sariah didn't say a word, as she nearly jumped into his arms and kissed his cheek to say thank you.

Leah saw the pleading eyes of Priscilla. She held out her hands inviting her into her arms. "Come here, my Priscilla girl", she said.

Priscilla smiled as Leah lifted the growing six-year-old to her hip.

Ezra surprised his mother by asking her, "Do you think Jesus is from God, like the prophets we learned about at synagogue?"

"I was wondering when he healed people, where did he get the power, and why?" Caleb asked.

"Don't you remember that a redeemer has been promised to come? Leah asked. "I believe that perhaps we have seen him."

"The Promised One?" Caleb exclaimed with shock in his voice.

Leah nodded her head, "That is what many are saying."

When they arrived home, the girls laid on mats to rest. Caleb sat on a mat, rubbing his arms, tired from carrying his sister.

Leah pulled out the small block of cheese with the rest of yesterday's bread. She poured the last of the pomegranate for the water.

Ezra said, "Momma I'll get some water." Then went out the door to the well.

After their meal, Leah tired and emotionally drained, said to her family, "It has been quite a day, hasn't it?"

All four of the children answered, "Yes."

Priscilla added, "Yes it has been, momma, we saw Jesus!"

Leah continued to pray to the Almighty God. She was more convinced that Jesus was sent by God. The same peace that she felt as she prayed was the same peace she had when Jesus looked at her.

Over the next few weeks, Leah's work continued to be difficult. She, alone, still carried the responsibility of providing for her children. Yet, since her encounter with Jesus, the hard work didn't drain her as it did before. She knew that she had to look to Jesus for strength, nowhere else.

One day, Leah stood amazed as she looked at the number of coins that were in her hand. It was payment for a complicated repair of a tapestry. It was much more than she had ever been paid for her work.

"You are a miracle worker, fixing that tapestry, I am going to tell others of your talents," said the head servant, who had given her the coins.

She didn't know how to respond to the compliment; she simply thanked the man. As she walked home, she remembered she must always look to Jesus.

Leah and the children continued to hear accounts of Jesus' activities. Caleb told them of Jesus raising a man back to life after he had been in the tomb for four days.

"Why didn't Jesus heal him before he died?" Caleb asked.

Leah responded by telling him, "Maybe, it was to prove his authority and power."

"I believe that Jesus has been sent by God," Caleb said. "But, I'm not sure if he is a prophet or the promised one."

Leah urged Caleb to talk with the Almighty God about these questions and anything else that he might have on his heart.

Soon, Leah began to notice that she was not as fatigued as before at the end of the day. She now was getting steady work. She was even able to get some new customers. When the money would run short, she remembered to look to Jesus. She knew that Jesus was able to care for her and her children. She would pray reminding herself to trust in God alone.

She often would be astonished at how things would work out — an extra job, or a gift of food, a neighbor giving clothing that their children had outgrown. There were so many ways that the answer would come. Leah began to be excited to watch how God was working.

A few months passed when a knock on the door to their humble room began to reveal a pathway for Leah and her family to experience freedom and provision that they never could have imagined.

When Leah opened the door she saw her father's brother. "Oh Uncle Simon, what a great surprise, we haven't seen you in so long," she said.

Uncle Simon looked at Leah and the children, then scanned the tiny room where the five of them lived. It had the barest of accommodations. There were simple mats rolled up in the corner for their beds, and a small table with a few cushions. There was only an outer robe on one peg. There was no bread, cheese or fruit for a meal.

He opened his arms to the children, as they came and greeted him. Soon the room was filled with conversation and laughter. After a while, the girls went to play with their handmade toys.

Uncle Simon called the boys over to him and handed them some coins.

"Let's have a celebration! Go to the market get three good-sized fish, bread, cheese and some figs," he directed. Make sure that there is enough for us all!"

Caleb and Ezra's eyes filled with excitement, and then Caleb said, "A celebration! I am on my way."

Leah was shocked as she listened to Uncle Simon send the boys to the market for food.

Uncle Simon helped her start a fire to cook the fish, and Leah fought the urge to cry. She was overwhelmed by the provision of the Lord. She had prayed this morning asking God to help bring food. She had no money left for food that day, and there was nothing left from yesterday.

Soon the boys arrived with all the items their uncle had requested; the fire was ready for the fish. Priscilla and Sariah carefully poured water into clay cups.

"Let's offer our thanksgiving to the Lord God Almighty," Uncle Simon said.

Caleb saw his momma wiping her eyes while their uncle prayed.

After the meal was eaten and cleaned up, the children all went outside.

Uncle Simon and Leah remained at the table. For a moment they enjoyed the quiet that came into the tiny room.

Uncle Simon looked to Leah and then began, "My dear niece, first I want to tell you I am so sorry that I didn't know that you have struggled so much, alone."

Leah could see that his eyes were moist and she heard the strain in his voice he spoke. When she saw her uncle's emotion, her eyes began to fill as well.

Uncle Simon began again, "Since your father is gone, as your father's brother, I should have helped you. I don't have much myself. But I believe if we can work together, I might have a solution for you and your family."

Leah's eyes grew large as he began to talk with her about a small piece of land with a small house. He continued that he wanted to sell it to her.

She grew uncomfortable as he spoke. Didn't he know that she barely had enough to feed her children? How could she ever have money to purchase land?

"Uncle Simon I am so grateful that you see our situation and the needs that we have, but I have no way to buy land. Leah said. "Some days I have no money to feed my children."

Uncle Simon rubbed his thick beard. Her crying made him feel awkward.

"Oh my child, do you know how I found you?"

Leah just shook her head, her emotions were still overwhelming her.

He continued, "I was sent to find a person to mend rugs, tapestry and curtains for the wealthy of the city. A head servant gave me your name. He told me that you mended a tapestry for his master's home."

Leah looked at him puzzled, then she asked, "How can that buy land?"

"I know where you can work, and I know where your talent is needed. This man has many customers that will pay for your work. You will receive better wages and not have to constantly look for new people," her uncle said.

Leah was cautious. She considered whether this is of the Lord or is this another empty promise?

"Uncle, can I go see the place?" Leah said timidly.

"Of course, I will take you to the shop, too!" Simon said. "Do you want to go now, or tomorrow?"

"Can we go today? There are a few hours left in the day. I have a job tomorrow." Leah answered as she tried to calm her heart.

Leah called for Caleb. She asked him to care for Ezra, Priscilla, and Sariah for a while. She needed to go with uncle Simon.

Uncle Simon and Leah walked first to the shop, she saw numerous rugs, curtains, and tapestries in one part of the shop for sale, and in another part were rugs and tapestries that were each hanging on a frame for repair.

Uncle Simon explained how she could work every day in the shop.

Then they walked down several streets to a small property with a small house with four rooms.

Leah's heart leaped within her when she saw it. She was afraid to think that she could live there. Is this a dream? A trap? Is it even possible?

Uncle Simon could see the concern on her face as she looked into the rooms. "I want you to have this place. As your uncle I wish I could give it to you, but I can't. But, if you work at the shop for a few months, you will be able to buy the land."

Leah stood in the house and trembled as she asked the question, "How much are you asking for this land?"

When Uncle Simon gave her the amount, she nearly fainted. There was a possibility, a hope that this could be true. He was asking for much less than the land was worth.

"Uncle, can I pray about this for a day or two?" Leah stammered.

"Yes of course," he responded.

Leah returned home. What she had just seen, and what her uncle talked with her about, was spinning in her mind. She was battling between hope and not to hope. For the next few days, Leah prayed asking God to guide her.

Uncle Simon returned a few days later, and Leah knew that she needed to work some things out.

Leah said, "Uncle, I believe that God has moved in your heart to make this home available for my family. I also know that I must prove to the owner of the shop that I can complete the work as they desire. So, I feel that I should work for the owner for the next month and not move until I know I can pay you for the property."

Uncle Simon could see that this was a good plan for her, and said to her, "You are a smart one, my girl. I think that you are making a wise plan."

He took Leah to meet the owner of the shop, and she began to work immediately.

Over the next month, she was able to make more money and was even able to save. But it was not enough to buy the property. She asked her uncle if he could wait until she had more saved. He understood that she was doing everything she could, and he agreed that he could wait a little longer.

Leah had saved almost enough to purchase the property. She needed another couple of months to have enough. Then her Uncle Simon came to tell her that he couldn't wait any longer.

Leah felt like her hopes and dreams were crushed, where was she going to get the remainder of the money for the property? Her uncle told her that he was sorry to pressure her, but she had until the end of the month, which was just a few days away.

Heartbroken, Leah asked all the children to go outside until sundown. She wanted to pray alone for a while. She went to the corner of the room and fell to her knees.

At first, she didn't have any words to begin to pray. The sense of disappointment that she felt was like someone had covered her mouth. Then a wave of sadness flooded her. She buried her face in her hands on the floor when she began weeping. Her whole body shook from the emotion, her weeping grew to a wail of pain; it was as if she was dying inside. She felt cold and utterly alone.

She continued to weep and wail until there was nothing left within her. She was exhausted, and her head hurt, yet everything was still the same. Even though her sobs subsided, the emptiness in her heart felt like she could not bear it any longer. Thoughts assailed her that she should give up, it would never happen no matter how hard she tried.

She remained on her knees, silent. Then she quieted her heart as much as she could. After a few moments, she felt a peace in the room. She had her eyes closed she and began to see the day that she took the children to see Jesus. She remembered the compassion he had for each of her children.

She heard the whisper in her ear, "Look to Jesus."

Leah responded to the whisper, "I will look to Jesus. I know I must trust in you; you will take care of us no matter what."

Leah got up from the floor soon after, not feeling defeated or discouraged any longer. She washed her face, and she remembered what Joshua said to the people, "Have I not commanded you? Be strong and courageous, do not be afraid; do not be discouraged, for the Lord your God will be with you wherever you go." (Joshua 1:9 NIV)

When the children entered the home near sundown, Leah had a meal prepared and a new strength within.

As the days passed, Leah refused to allow desperation to take hold. But sometimes worry wriggled into her thoughts. She would say in a whisper, "Look to Jesus."

On the last day, Leah prayed and thanked the Lord for all he had done for her. She thanked God for being able to save money, she was thankful for her job, for her children seeing Jesus, and for all the many ways that she has watched God at work.

When she was ready to go home at the end of her workday, the shop owner came to her. He told her what a talent she had, and the good work she had done for his customers. Then told her that he was aware of the land and home that was being offered. He also knew that she did not have all the money needed to complete the purchase.

Leah nodded, but did not say a word, within herself, she said, "Look to Jesus."

The owner told her that he would give her the needed amount and that she could pay him as she worked.

Leah was shocked, she realized that God was working through others in so many different ways to bring this to pass. Her tears began to flow freely. She knew that God wanted her to only trust in him.

Over the next few days, Uncle Simon and Leah worked on the documentation for the property to belong to her and her family.

She had not told her children anything about the possibility of the property. At times she thought she would burst with worry, with hope, with despair, and then with the great news. She waited until it was done. On the day that all of the legalities were completed, Leah took her four children for a walk. She could hardly contain the excitement and joy that was in her.

Caleb asked as they walked down an unfamiliar street, "Where are we going, Momma?"

Leah answered, "I want to take you to a special place."

Ezra and the girls looked at the houses as they walked, they pointed out the ones that drew their attention.

Ezra said, "Momma, do you think we will ever have a house?'

Leah answered, "I have been praying for that for years. Over the past months, since we went to see Jesus, God has been showing me, that I can't look to anyone but Jesus. I must look to him for everything!"

Just then, Leah walked up to a gate and put a key in the lock, while four sets of eyes were in shock as she opened the gate to a patio. They followed her to the door where she opened the front door.

Leah waited for her children to come into the house, and then she said, "Let's join hands and pray. Dear God, Almighty, you have shown me that you are faithful, you are our loving father. You reminded me to be courageous and bold, not to fear or be discouraged. You know the needs and the desires of our hearts. You know the best ways to meet all of our needs and desires and even things we don't know we need. I ask that we always remain grateful to you. I know your Mercy is everlasting."

When they finished their prayer, Ezra looked at his mother and then asked, "Why are we here?"

Leah trying to control the emotion in her voice, answered, "Because, I wanted to bring you home."

Chapter 6

THE WITNESS

When the centurion and those with him

who were guarding Jesus saw the earthquake

and all that had happened,

they were terrified, and exclaimed,

"Surely he was the Son of God!"

Matthew 27:54 NIV

Early in the morning, Lucius received a summons to the court of Pontius Pilate for a meeting. He excitedly readied himself for the meeting as he hoped that the summons was regarding his request for a transfer to a different area. As Lucius walked through the streets, he wondered where he might be sent. The Roman Empire was vast, and there were regions in all directions.

Lucius felt a sense of awe as he caught sight of Herod's Palace, and it thrilled him each time he entered the palace compound. The architecture was magnificent. The colonnade of pillars supporting the ornate arches created a gateway to the colorfully paved outer court. The majestic buildings at either end of the court displayed Rome's power and authority. One building was the residence of Pontius Pilate. The other was the praetorium.

Lucius reflected on how grateful he was that he was born a Roman. He was honored to be a soldier and serve Emperor Tiberius. He had traveled much and was acquainted with battle. He had witnessed first hand the cruelty of humanity. He understood his purpose, authority, and power. Lucius was proud to be a Roman soldier. He had worked his way through the ranks from the lowest legionary to the level of centurion, a commander of 100 men. But Lucius had his sights set even higher.

Lucius was accustomed to military campaigns and battles, but for the past few years, he has been stuck in Judea. It was filled with sheep herders, fishermen, and Jews. He could not understand the Jewish way of living with their strict laws, dress, and customs. He wanted to experience more of the world. He hoped that he would finish his career by being sent somewhere more important than with the Jews in Judea.

When he arrived at the palace, a court soldier led him to the praetorium, then to an area to wait for Pilate to call him. From where Lucius waited, he had a clear view of the activity in the court and the throne of Pilate. He stood leaning against the wall, while he watched three men addressing Pontius Pilate. He noticed their fine colorful garments over a white tunic. He knew at once, that they were Jewish temple priests.

He he recognized the one talking with Pontius Pilate was the high priest of the temple, Caiaphas. Lucius could see the intense look on Caiphas' face as spoke to Pilate, who sat comfortably on his throne listening. The two men with Caiaphas stood silently on either side of him. Lucius became more interested in their conversation as he could see Caiaphas growing more animated as he continued. Then he overheard part of the discussion between Caiaphas and Pilate. He was talking about the man from Nazareth.

He knew the Nazarene had been trouble for Caiaphas for the past three years. Lucius had been aware of the man from Nazareth from the crowds that followed him. He did not seem like an extremist or an activist, but with his teachings he could hold the attention of a crowd of thousands for hours.

This man, Jesus, had been traveling all over Judea with his message to the people. The Jewish leadership was watching Jesus closely, and they had labeled him a heretic, trying to stop his influence.

As Lucius watched Caiaphas before Pilate, he saw Pilate motion for his soldier near the throne and spoke to him. Lucius watched as Pilate looked his way. At that moment he knew that he was not going to get a transfer.

Instantly, irritation welled up within him as the servant indicate for Lucius to approach Pilate. Lucius hesitated for a second thinking the Jewish priests would leave. The servant noticed his pause and again motioned for him to proceed to Pilate.

The soldier saluted with a right-hand clenched fist over the heart, and said, "Centurion Lucius as requested."

Lucius saluted Pilate and waited for his address.

Pilate readjusted himself on his throne. He now sat upright with an air of annoyance, as he looked at Caiaphas and then at Lucius.

"Caiaphas, this is Centurion Lucius," Pilate said with authority. "He will be assigned to Jerusalem and be focused on the temple area to help with the crowds."

He then waved his hand indicating that the visit was over. Caiaphas bowed and thanked Pilate for his help then began to leave the throne area. Lucius was frustrated that he was not able to express his desire to transfer to another area. Now he was assigned to the Jews, and this is not what he wanted for his life as a centurion.

Trying to control his emotions about this assignment, Lucius saluted Pilate. He then turned and made his way to speak with Caiaphas. He told Caiaphas he would visit him at the temple later in the afternoon. As the soldier led them out of the Palace, they remained silent. Lucius turned in the opposite direction of Caiaphas, to make his way back to his quarters. With each step, he felt infuriated that he was now trapped in Jerusalem. Lucius briskly walked down the hallway towards his quarters. Even though he tried to hide his frustration and disappointment, the dark scowl on his face communicated it.

He slammed the door when he entered the common room of the officer's quarters, and the noise was heard all over. Cassius, who was sitting across the room at his desk, looked up trying to hide the smirk, and asked Lucius, "Did the meeting with Pilate go well?"

"No! The meeting did not go well, Cassius." Lucius answered, trying not to shout. Then more calmly he said, "I thought, when I was summoned it was to see Pilate was about my transfer out of Judea."

"I have been moved from general peacekeeping throughout Judea to be assigned to Jerusalem focused on the Jewish temple," Lucius said through clinched teeth.

Cassius answered with a questioning look, "Jerusalem I understand, but to focus on the temple? Is Caiaphas upset about the Nazarene again?"

Lucius, pacing the floor from agitation, slowed to a stop as he responded , "I did overhear several comments about him when Caiaphas was talking with Pilate. He has been troubling for Caiaphas, but not for Rome. This is for the Jews to work out, not Roman soldiers."

Lucius greeted Caiaphas later in the day at the temple in a private area. Caiaphas took charge by saying, "Lucius, we want to thank you for your help in this very delicate, yet important, matter. There is a man called Jesusof Nazareth. He teaches heresies and creates unrest within the Jewish community."

Lucius listened to the high priest carefully, then asked, "I know that the Nazarene draws great crowds of people wherever he goes. I have had no reports of unrest or hostility in the gatherings."

Caiaphas responded in a more defensive tone, "He breaks our laws and defies our teachings, he is gaining popularity and a following!"

Lucius replied coldly to Caiaphas, "I will be watchful of the Nazarene and his followers as I have been instructed, here in Jerusalem and the temple."

Caiaphas returned to the temple and Lucius went back to his quarters.

Lucius pondered whether this Jesus from Nazareth was really a threat as Caiaphas says, or just a man who would soon fade away. In his duties over the past years, Lucius had only minimal information regarding Jesus. Over the next few days, Lucius spoke with the people of Jerusalem about Jesus of Nazareth.

He was surprised by one response from a man who told him that Jesus was raised in Nazareth and had been a carpenter until he was 30 years of age. He then set out on his endeavor. Lucius began to think, how could a simple carpenter be such a threat to the power of the priest and traditions of the Jews?

He was increasingly perplexed by the comments from the people in Jerusalem, his messages did not speak against Rome or their rule. Through his years he had seen other worshippers of deities or fanatics of all types that never generated trouble like this.

One evening as he sat in the common room, a centurion that he did not know sat nearby. The man nervously wrung his hands.

"How go you?" Lucius greeted the man as a fellow centurion.

The centurion began haltingly, "I am Remus assigned to the area of Capernaum. I was told that you have been assigned to Jerusalem and over the temple. Because of Jesus of Nazareth."

Lucius calmly nodded at Remus.

"Yes, the priests are complaining to Pontius Pilate, so here I am."

Remus looked at Lucius, took a deep breath, then gazed out to the window as he struggled to start, "I came to Jerusalem for a meeting. But when I heard of your assignment, I wanted to come and talk with you.

"In Capernaum, Jesus is often in the area with his disciples and followers. I regularly monitored the very large crowds that came to hear him. I would listen to the messages he would give to the multitudes, and I watched as people would come to him that were lame, blind, and extremely ill."

Remus stopped for a moment, cleared his throat, rubbed his hands together and started again, "Jesus performed miracles."

Lucius held up his hand to interrupt him, then asked, "What do you mean miracles?"

Remus looked at his hands then said, "He would go up to each one of the people, then Jesus would just touch them, and the lame would walk, the blind would see, and the sick were healed."

Lucius watched Remus as he grew silent, on Remus' face you could see this was emotional for him to share. Lucius waited as Remus collected himself to speak.

"About a year ago, my servant of many years and much favored by me was gravely ill. I knew there was nothing more that could be done for him. "When I was notified, that Jesus had just returned to the area, I requested Jewish leaders to go and ask Jesus to heal my servant. The men went to Jesus on my behalf. As the men were bringing Jesus to my home and were near, I knew that I was not worthy for him to come to my home. I sent friends to Jesus to tell him not to trouble himself to come, to just say the word and my servant would be healed."

Remus slowed his speech, then said with a tremble, "Before the men returned to my home, my servant was healed. Jesus healed my servant without coming to my house, without touching him. He just gave the word."

Remus looked up to Lucius as he finished speaking, waiting for Lucius' reaction.

"Thank you for coming and for that information," Remus. "Do you believe this man, Jesus, to be a threat to Rome?"

Remus was surprised by the question.

"Do I believe Jesus is a threat to Rome? No. Is he a threat to the Jews? Yes. His messages challenge them."

Lucius held up his hand for him to stop then responded coldly, "That is what I needed to know, the Jews are not my concern."

Remus's face showed the shock and surprise he felt. He politely thanked Lucius for his time and left.

The following morning Lucius was finalizing the placement of the soldiers for the crowds coming into the city for the Feast, when there was a loud knock on the door. His servant, a bit breathless, told him Jesus was coming from Bethany toward Jerusalem, and that many people were following him. Lucius went out the door and and headed in the direction of the temple.

Looking down the street that led to the temple, he could see the crowds of people that had lined the street. Then he saw a man on a donkey. He hurried closer, to get a better view. The people were putting palm branches and their cloaks on the ground where the donkey walked with Jesus. He was astonished that the people were singing, and waving the palm branches. The people were from all segments of society.

He stood watching as the people sang, "Blessed is he who comes in the name of the Lord. Blessed is the King of Israel!"

He was stunned as he heard them say, "King of Israel."

"This man is the King of Israel?" Lucius silently questioned. "He has no authority, or power, not even an army. All I see are worshippers of no consequence."

He continued to watch; to personally assess this man, Jesus of Nazareth. While the mass of people made their way to the temple to worship. As he watched Jesus, he noticed that all types of people were able to come up to him, and he would speak to them. Even though there were men who were with Jesus, they did not hinder or restrain the people from addressing him. Lucius was amazed when he saw Greek men speaking with Jesus.

He continued to look through the crowd and spotted a group of Jewish priests speaking to one another. Lucius recognized one of them who had stood with Caiaphas at the palace.

Lucius laughed then thought, "Yes, this Jesus of Nazareth is a threat to them. They are losing their followers to Jesus."

As Lucius walked through the crowd, he questioned whether they had come to celebrate the Feast or for Jesus. Finally, Lucius called for a soldier, gave an order to monitor the people and to get him word if any problem were to arise. He then made his way back to his quarters.

The next morning Lucius was interrupted by his soldier who came to him with excited energy. He stopped before him, saluting quickly, "Sir, the man Jesus is creating a ruckus at the temple."

Lucius grabbed his sheathed sword and strapped it to his waist. His steps toward the temple were brisk, covering the distance quickly. When he arrived at the temple, he found he had to force his way through a mass of people.

"What is happening, I was told Jesus of Nazareth is creating trouble," Lucius asked a guard near the temple.

"Jesus came from Bethany to the Temple," the guard said. "As soon as he entered the turmoil began. He started by driving out those that were buying and selling. He overturned the table of the money changer and stands where the doves were sold. When the merchants began to shout at Jesus for disrupting their sales, some Pharisees came out from another area and, in their rush, turned over a table of a merchant. Which created even more commotion in the temple."

"Jesus then stood before everyone and said, 'It is written, my house will be called a house of prayer, but you have made it a den of thieves.'"

"But sir." the soldier continued,. "What happened next was unbelievable. The blind and lame went to him, and Jesus healed them. Children began shouting in the temple 'Hosanna to the Son of David.' I could see the chief priest and other religious leaders were indignant."

Lucius asked, "Did he steal any items or money, or did he strike anyone?"

The soldier answered, "No, not that I saw and not that anyone has told me."

Lucius then smiled as he asked, "Did Jesus of Nazareth take any tribute of any kind for these miracles of healing?" If so, Lucius thought Jesus could be guilty of not paying taxes.

The soldier thought for a moment then responded, "No, after they were healed, they praised their God and left happy."

"As far as you saw or was reported to you, this Jesus has not broken any Roman law. So, has it all been squabbles about the Jews' rules and customs?" Lucius asked with obvious frustration.

"Continue monitoring Jesus' activities and the crowd, until your replacement comes," Lucius said, as he turned on his heel and walked back through the streets from the temple.

Lucius was increasingly frustrated by the assignment and began to think to himself, "I am a centurion with one hundred men under my command, and I am watching a single man, a carpenter from Nazareth. I know how to lead men into battle. If something does not come of this conflict between the religious leaders and Jesus, this could ruin my career."

Over the following days, Lucius was informed daily by the soldiers of Jesus' movements in the area. Jesus would pass the day at the temple, then leave Jerusalem at night to return to Bethany. The following morning he would return to Jerusalem and the temple. One soldier described the great number of people who would seek him out and then listen intently to what Jesus would say.

Another soldier also commented that the high priest and other religious leaders were constantly nearby listening to Jesus' message as well. Several of the religious leaders spoke to Jesus and at times had discussions with him, trying to entrap him.

Lucius grew more annoyed, even though the conflict between Jesus and the religious leaders was reaching a crisis. He reminded himself that their controversy and disagreements had nothing to do with Rome. This is a Jewish problem he repeated to himself. His exasperation with being assigned to this menial quarrel between the Jewish leadership and a simple man angered him. He had Roman soldiers, who were battle seasoned, trained for combat, sent to watch Jesus' every move, make note of who he spoke with, and where he went. What is the Jewish leadership going to do about him? He thought seriously. They have no authority to put anyone to death. That can only be ordered by Pontius Pilate.

Lucius knew that the temple leadership and priests were devising a plan to eliminate the problem of the Nazarene. He had seen the hostility from the high priest Caiaphas and other leaders, toward Jesus. But he had no idea how they would go about it. So in the meantime, there would be more soldiers watching and more reports to be made. Lucius was becoming bitter about how these Jews, with their traditions, laws, and internal arguments, have disrupted his plans.

The next day Lucius walked through the main streets in Jerusalem. They were bustling the Jewish residents preparing for the Passover. He was amazed at how the city's population swelled from the arrival of the countless travelers who had come for these special days. He considered what orders would need to be put in place with so many devoted Jews coming to the temple to worship. Lucius commanded an increase of patrols of soldiers in the streets, market areas and near the temple. Other soldiers would continue to monitor the religious leaders and Jesus.

Lucius observed the crowds as he walked through the busiest market areas, where people were at every stand filling their baskets with the items for their special meals for Passover. Under a large olive tree, the shade provided a place for a group of women in simple clothing to greet each other. Nearby their children were running and playing. He could hear a mother call out to one of the children to stay close.

As he walked a little further, he noticed, at the corner, several men listening to one man who was dressed in priestly clothing. The man was talking with much emotion.

Finally, Lucius walked toward the temple to complete his circuit to assess if there would be a need to change his orders. There were crowds at the temple, many were travelers, but he did not see Jesus or his disciples. He thought that the stronger military presence might be helping to maintain order throughout the city and the temple area.

The hour was growing late as he returned to his quarters. As he sat down, he smiled and thought, "The Jews should be busy with their activities tonight, and soldiers are patrolling the whole city."

Some short time later, a sense of restlessness grew within him. He stood and moved to the window to look out over the city. As the sun passed the horizon, the evening grew darker, the buildings became just a shadowy outline from where he stood.

Suddenly, throughout the city, flickers of a golden glow began to shine from homes throughout the areas of the city of Jerusalem. Lucius remained at the window staring out, as the glow from the homes kept the city from being completely enveloped by the darkness of the night. As time passed the sounds of people faded as many homes quieted for a night to rest and then to awake to celebrate the Jewish holy festival.

When he yawned it drew his attention away from the scene from the window. He retired to his room to rest and forget about Jesus, the temple, and the contentious religious leaders.

Not long before dawn, Lucius' sleep was interrupted by the sounds of men calling to him as they entered his quarters. As an experienced soldier, Lucius was awake, up, and wanting information regarding their presence before they were allowed to enter his bed chambers.

The first soldier saluted Lucius and then said, "Sir, there is trouble. Caiaphas has arrested Jesus!"

Another soldier added, "They have taken him to Annas' house, he is the father-in-law of Caiaphas. The religious council of the temple has had a meeting."

Even though Lucius was surprised, he knew this was serious. The temple priests had waited until nightfall on one of their holiest days.

"Let's go! Take me there, now!" Lucius said with his commanding voice.

They had not even traveled to the end of the street, when another soldier running toward them spoke quickly, "Sir, the temple guards and priests are taking the Nazarene to Pilate!"

Changing direction his entourage headed toward praetorium. Lucius knew that Jews would ask Pilate to put Jesus to death. His pace was quick; he needed to be there before

Caiaphas and his crowd arrived from the temple. He wanted to be there first and to have his men in place. These Jews were out for Jesus' blood.

Lucius observed the sunrise. He knew that Pilate's day normally would not begin before the third hour. There was much to assess and prepare. These are the very people that he was assigned to monitor.

As Lucius rounded the corner to the pathway that entered the praetorium. He noticed that a crowd was in the waiting area where grievances were heard and ruled on by Pontius Pilate. He was surprised at how many were there so early to secure a place in line.

The early morning calm was broken by the noise of the men bringing Jesus to Pontius Pilate. As they entered the Praetorium, Lucius was stunned by the size of the group of men accompanying Jesus. He then realized that it had to be the whole Sanhedrin, comprising more than seventy men who had brought Jesus.

There were two temple guards in front of Jesus, one on either side, and two walking behind him. Jesus' hands were bound, his face was bruised. His eyes were red and swollen, and his lips and nose were bleeding. Jesus was silent and made no resistance when he entered. The temple guards handed Jesus off to the palace guards, who guided him to a holding cell near the platform.

Following the men of the Sanhedrin were many people. It was evident that they were curious to know what was happening. The palace courtyard was quickly filled with people and soon there was a buzz of conversation regarding why the whole Sanhedrin had brought Jesus of Nazareth to Pontius Pilate.

Lucius was quickly surveyed the security for the area, then he motioned for soldiers to take positions at the front for protection of Pilate. He directed other soldiers to be along the perimeter of all those that had come. He knew this had the makings for a volatile scene. He wanted the military presence to be seen and felt by all those who were in the courtyard.

A soldier came up to Lucius to relay that Pilate wanted him to report to him on the platform. He quickly obeyed and was standing near the throne. He saluted Pilate when he stood before him. Lucius could see that Pilate seemed agitated as he looked to Jesus and then to the crowd.

"The Jews come in force today against the man Jesus," Pilate said to Lucius. "We shall see what happens."

As Lucius stood facing the crowd, he observed that nearly all those present in the court were men from the temple council.

"Yes, I see that most of the people here are opponents of the Nazarene," Lucius said. "The rest of the people arrived by intrigue."

Pilate said nothing to Lucius or his advisors for several moments as he observed the people in the courtyard.

A thought came to Lucius, as he surveyed those who were present.

"Where are his followers?" Shaking his head slightly the thoughts continued, "Mmm, at first sign of physical threat or trouble, they are gone! Where is their loyalty?"

Lucius noticed the men in priestly garments were moving through the crowd, talking with those who followed them in.

Pilate sighed deeply then looked to Lucius and nodded his head to indicate that he was ready to begin.

Jesus, with hands bound, was brought onto the platform. There was a guard on either side of him. Lucius considered Jesus' demeanor and his appearance as he walked onto the platform. Even though he had been beaten, Jesus was calm and quiet. Lucius noted that he was not nervous at all. Normally, when men were in this situation, they were anxious, nervous and fearful.

Pilate looked to the priests and then asked, "Why is this man before me?"

Two priests stepped out of the temple leadership assembly and began to speak at the same time, accusing Jesus by saying, "We have found this man trying to subvert the nation. He also opposes payment of taxes to Cesar, and he claimed to be Christ the king."

Pilate looked over to Lucius, questioning the validity of the accusations of the priests regarding Rome.

"Jesus, are you King of the Jews?" Pilate asked.

"Yes, it is as you say," Jesus responded,

The Roman leader asked other questions but found no substance to accusations against Jesus. Pilate was growing frustrated.

Lucius observed the high priests and temple leaders as they continued to claim Jesus had stirred up the people all over Judea and here in Jerusalem.

Pilate motioned for Lucius to come close so they could speak privately.

"Have you found anything that supports their accusations?" Pilate asked.

"Sir, I have diligently inquired with many locally as well as the centurion assigned to the Capernaum sector and have found nothing," Lucius whispered to the ruler.

"He incites people all over Judea with his teaching," a temple leader shouted out. "It began in Galilea and has come to Jerusalem."

Pilate moved in his seat after hearing that statement. He knew that Jesus was under Herod's authority. Fortunately, Herod just happened to be in Jerusalem.

"Lucius, take him to Herod," Pilate said with relief in his voice.

When Lucius took Jesus to Herod, the whole of the Sanhedrin followed along.

When Jesus was led before Herod, Lucius noticed the obvious look of pleasure on Herod's face. A nearby guard explained to Lucius that Herod had been curious about wanting to see Jesus perform miracles. Lucius witnessed the eagerness of Herod as he began to question Jesus. Regardless of the question, Jesus did not respond or react to Herod.

Lucius inwardly chuckled as it was no surprise that Herod soon grew exasperated and angry at the lack of response by Jesus.

While Herod was questioning Jesus, the chief priests, and other temple leaders were relentless in their accusations against Jesus. The men of the Sanhedrin were shouting out to Herod their claims of Jesus' crimes against Rome.

Herod, weary from the noise from the religious men, as well as Jesus' indifference to him, allowed his soldiers to mock and beat him and humiliate him. Herod then sent him back to Pilate.

Once again Lucius directed his soldiers to begin the trip back to Pilate. Behind him were the men of the Sanhedrin, and many others that were spectators to this event.

Lucius watched the man called Jesus. He was calm and controlled, which surprised him. He marveled at his courage and strength because Lucius knew Jesus was facing death.

"The news of Jesus' arrest must have made its way through town," Lucius thought as he returned to the praetorium because the courtyard was filling to overflowing.

The guards led Jesus in front of the judgment seat, while Lucius spoke privately with Pilate regarding Herod's dismissal of Jesus.

Immediately the men began to shout accusations against Jesus again. Pilate watched and listened to them, as he considered his options. Pilate held up his hand to silence everyone and then motioned for Jesus to be brought closer.

"What say you to these charges against you?" Pilate asked. Jesus stood not responding in any way.

"Do you hear their testimony against you?" Pilate asked. Still, Jesus remained silent.

Pilate shifted in his seat, a movement that was from frustration. He found no fault in the man, but Jesus was not helping himself.

Pilate motioned for a palace guard to have Jesus move aside, and asked to have a guard to come to him.

Again, the men began to shout, but Pilate, once again, held up a hand for silence.

"I have found no basis for your charges against him, Pilate said. "Neither did Herod find anything, that is why he was sent back. He has done nothing deserving of death. Therefore, I will punish him and then release him."

Shouting erupted immediately, with the same claims, yet this time more men had joined in with the Sanhedrin.

A palace guard approached Pilate and then waited for permission to come close. Frustrated by the interruption he waved him over. The noise from commotion from the courtyard required the guard to speak loudly to Pilate.

Lucius heard the guard tell Pilate that the message was from his wife. She had a dream that had caused her great suffering. She warned Pilate not to have anything to do with this just man, because he had been brought to him through envy.

Pilate responded with a deep sigh and then motioned for the guard to step away.

Lucius could see the concern sweep over Pilate's face as another commotion erupted. Men were yelling and chains were rattling, as four palace guards were struggling with a man to bring him onto the platform.

There was an audible gasp from the people to see the infamous prisoner Barabbas. He had been imprisoned for insurrection and murder.

There was an uncomfortable moment that passed over the crowd. Then the murmur could be heard among the people.

Lucius looked over to the two men standing bound between guards. He noticed a contrast between the two men. The man Jesus was guiltless of the charges that were being presented. Barabbas was known for his brutality and murder and his insurrection against Rome.

Again, Pilate raised his hand to gain the attention of everyone in the praetorium, then he stood and strode closer to the end of the platform.

"It is the governor's custom at this Feast to release a prisoner by the choice of the people," Pilate announced.

Lucius thought that the people would certainly select Jesus.

But, immediately and nearly in unison, the courtyard rang with voices saying, "Release Barabbas to us! We want Barabbas!"

Lucius was stunned by the that reaction.

"Wasn't it just a few days ago, that people waved palms, spread their cloaks, and sang to this Jesus?" Lucius thought to himself. "Now they have chosen a murderer, Barabbas over Jesus.

He remembered being told that Jesus had healed the lame, and restored sight to the blind. Now they turn so quickly against him?

"I just do not understand Jews."

Lucius watched Pilate pace across the platform as he grew more frustrated and agitated. It was obvious that Pilate wanted to release Jesus.

As Pilate appealed to them again, the crowd began to shout with more hostility, "Crucify him! Crucify him!"

Pilate stood in the center of the platform glaring at the group of priests and people in the courtyard, then said, "Why? What is his crime, what has this

man done? I have no grounds that are deserving of his death, I will punish him and then release him."

Suddenly loud shouts from the courtyard overpowered the voice of Pilate. The crowd demanded that Jesus be crucified. The shouting continued and grew in intensity until Pilate decided to permit their demands.

He walked over to a table that held a pitcher and bowl. Pilate poured water over his hands and then spoke to the bloodthirsty crowd, "I am innocent of this man's blood, it is by your request."

"Let it be on us and our children," answered the crowd.

With the weight of what would come, Pilate nodded slowly at Lucius and orders ere given to release Barabbas, and to hand Jesus over to the palace guards to be flogged and then crucified.

"Lucius, you oversee, everything," Pilate ordered as he left the platform.

Lucius followed the palace guards to a corner of the praetorium. He leaned against the wall near the guards. He saw a look of hardness in the company of soldiers encircling Jesus. The men laughed as they stripped him, spit on him, and with a staff, hit him repeatedly on the head.

Aware that the assignment to Pilate's palace was desired by many, Lucius knew the soldiers who had trained for battle were often bored with their menial duties there. Perhaps today would help relieve their boredom and restlessness, but it would be at an innocent man's expense.

The soldiers took the bound hands of Jesus and tied them to a post. A larger muscular soldier retrieved a whip with chips of bone in the ends. As the guard neared the post where Jesus was tied, he handed his cloak to another guard, raised his arm, swinging the whip down, lashing the exposed back of Jesus. The slap of the whip was heard over and over as the chips of bone ripped into his flesh tearing it away and leaving gaping wounds. Yet only sounds from Jesus were grunts of pain.

The long lengths of the straps along with the force would whip around to the front of his body and face. Soon his whole body showed the deep gouges and the devastating brutality of the flogging.

The guards encircling the scene were watching. They counted each slap of the whip. They laughed, each asking to take a turn.

Lucius realized that not once did Jesus beg for them to stop, he took each lash with courage.

Finally, Lucius yelled, "Stop! That is enough!"

The guard who administered most of the whipping sat down exhausted and requested a drink as he began to rub his arm and shoulder.

When another guard released Jesus from the post, he slumped into a heap on the ground. An eager guard grabbed Jesus roughly and jerked him to his feet. He was barely able to stand when they placed a robe on his bloody body.

Another guard came with a crown of thorny vines, and said, "Don't forget your crown," then forced it down onto Jesus' head.

Peels of laughter began as the guards all began to bow down and in mockery saying, "Hail to the King of the Jews!" They spit on him and hit him. One guard repeatedly grabbed a handful of his beard and pulled it out. Then another guard ripped the robe from him which wrenched pieces of flesh and caused renewed bleeding, and with gasps of pain, Jesus fell to the ground.

Lucius once again stopped them by saying, "Don't kill him before we crucify him."

"Do you have your tools here?" Lucius asked.

A guard lifted three long nails and a hammer in his hands for Lucius to see, "Yes, Sir!" he said.

Jesus was yanked to his feet by two guards. He was then pushed to begin to walk. He was struggling to balance himself when another guard pulled hard on the binding around his wrists, and he fell face-first on the pavement.

As laughter erupted from the guards, he was jerked to his feet again.

"Stop!" Lucius shouted at the men while a feeling of disgust grew within him.

"Let us get this over with, take him out onto the street," he commanded. Lucius could see that, Jesus was stumbling trying to walk, and his eyes were nearly swollen shut. Lucius assessed Jesus' condition, he realized how weak he was from the beatings. Jesus was not going to carry his cross all the way to Golgotha.

He looked over the crowd and then noticed a very muscular man who appeared to be from Cyrene. He sent one of the guards, to force the man from Cyrene to carry the cross behind Jesus.

Lucius had guards clear a pathway for Jesus and the man from Cyrene to walk. The streets were packed with people who had traveled to Jerusalem for the holy days.

People were pushed aside by the guards as crowds watched Jesus, a condemned man, walk toward Golgotha.

The number of spectators grew as they followed the procession of guards, Jesus, and the Jewish council.

When Jesus arrived at Golgotha, Lucius oversaw everything, as the guards began their duties for the crucifixion. The first guard offered Jesus a mixture of wine with gall, and after tasting it, he refused it.

Lucius was surprised that Jesus refused the drink, it was to help with the pain.

Another guard stripped him, then others laid him on the cross. Leather straps were tightly wound around the crossbeam and his arms to ensure no movement when the nails were to be driven into his hands. Then more leather straps were tightly wound around his legs and feet on the long beam and then his feet were nailed to the small block on the cross.

As Lucius listened to the hammering of the nails, and the grunts of pain from Jesus, he noticed there was no cursing or screams for mercy.

Lucius began to reflect on the many crucifixions he had witnessed in his career, and something seemed to be different about this one. Lucius felt as though there was something more going on, which unsettled him. He looked over to the men of the Sanhedrin, they appeared to be pleased.

They were talking among themselves. To Lucius, it looked like they were congratulating each other. Lucius felt nausea sweep over him.

"Ready sir!" a guard said.

Lucius walked over to the cross where Jesus had been nailed. He looked at both hands and then to his feet, to ensure that he was securely nailed. Lucius then gave the word to continue.

A guard brought a plaque that had the charge against him on it. It said, "This is the King of The Jews." He nailed it on the top of the cross. A silence fell over Golgotha as the guards moved into position.

Lucius signaled the men to begin lifting.

A voice shouted, "Up!'

The company of guards positioned at the top of the cross began to lift, while the rest of the guards steadied it. As the cross was lifted, the bottom of the beam slid into the hole and then slammed into place.

Breaking the silence, were the loud grunts, gasps, and groans from Jesus with every movement of the cross.

The cross swayed back and forth as the guards pounded thick pieces of wood around the base of the cross to lock it into place.

In the area where the guards sat to watch over the scene, Lucius noticed that several guards were casting lots to divide up Jesus' clothes. Those guards would gamble over anything.

Soon the hum of conversations and movement of people resumed on Golgotha as they settled to watch Jesus die.

People would walk by Jesus and shout at him with insults.

"You said you were going to destroy the temple then rebuild it in three days," one man said. Others mocked saying, "Save yourself, come down from there, if you are the Son of God!"

Lucius watched the chief priests begin to gather at the cross. He could see a triumphant look on their faces. One of the priests spoke almost in a shout speaking to the other priests, "He could save others, but he cannot save himself! He is the King of the Jews, let him come down from the cross, then we will believe."

A teacher of the law joined in with the insults saying, "He trusts in God, let God rescue him now if he wants him. Didn't he say, he was the Son of God?"

Lucius watched and listened to the vicious insults and contempt of the temple leadership toward Jesus. Again Lucius shook his head as he thought, "I do not understand the Jews."

Jesus remained silent the entire time, not answering the questions, taunts, or insults. Lucius could see Jesus looking over the people on Golgotha. He would push on the block where his feet were nailed so he could take a breath.

Lucius was Jesus began to speak. It was stunning to hear Jesus say, "Father, forgive them they do not know what they are doing."

"Who forgives the people who are putting you to death?" Lucius thought. "Who is this man?"

He began to contemplate what he had learned about Jesus over the past weeks. Jesus was unlike anyone he had ever encountered. Jesus did not try to make people follow him. He healed people without wanting anything in return. His messages were about being a better person. His only act of disturbance was at the temple when he threw the money changers and vendors out. He told them that the temple was to be a house of prayer. Lucius wondered if Jesus was here for a purpose.

As he meditated on these thought as he scanned the people there on Golgotha. He observed a group of women and a man who were weeping together. He observed how they agonized as they watched Jesus struggle for each breath. Lucius though they must be family.

The insults and mocking began again by many on the hill.

Unexpectedly, Lucius heard one of the criminals also suffering on a cross taunt Jesus.

"Aren't you the Christ, save yourself and us!"

The crowd grew quiet when they heard the other criminal respond rebuking his cohort, "Don't you fear God? We are under the same punishment. Our penalty is just and deserving. But this man has done nothing wrong."

That thief asked Jesus directly, "Will you remember me when you enter into your kingdom?"

Lucius staring at the three men on the cross, listened to Jesus answer the thief , "I tell you the truth, today you will be with me in paradise."

Again, Lucius asked himself, "Who is this man? What is he talking about, paradise? Why would Jesus answer the thief?"

Lucius had a mixture of feelings regarding Jesus. His thoughts were wrestling. He was very different from the other Jews, as well as other men, but why? He watched Jesus struggle to get a breath.

Jesus looked at the older woman in the small group. In a weak voice, he said, "Dear woman here is your son."

After another push on the block with his feet, to get a breath, Jesus looked at a young man in the group and then said haltingly, "Here is your mother."

The young man nodded to Jesus, then moved over to the woman. As Lucius watched the whole scene, he noticed how Jesus had relaxed as he gave her to the younger man, to ensure that the woman, who must have been his mother, was cared for from now on.

Thoughts raced through Lucius' mind, "What is all this, who is this man?" From the cross, he was concerned about his mother. Never in all my years has there ever been a man like this one."

Lucius saw Jesus' compassion for his mother, and the other criminal that was dying on a nearby cross. He knew this man was extraordinary. He remembered that he had questioned so many people about Jesus, that no one spoke against him other than the lies from the temple leaders.

Lucius was more conflicted, as he reviewed the past weeks. Then looked up to see the sun was high in the sky. He rubbed his temples as more and more thoughts came pouring in, "Was he sent here for a reason?"

He remembered the question from Pilate asking him under oath if he was Christ the Son of God. Jesus responded, that yes, he was the Son of God. "But was he the Son of God?" Lucius questioned.

The sound of Jesus' voice was but a whisper when he said, "I'm thirsty."

Lucius knew that Jesus was close to death, he saw a guard take a soaked sponge on a hyssop branch to Jesus. After he took a drink, he said with the last of his strength, "It is finished. Father, into your hands, I commit my Spirit."

A sense of ache filled Lucius, that he could not explain. He knew that Jesus had died. He said in a whisper, "Surely this man was the Son of God."

Astonished by his own words, he had called him the Son of God! Within himself, he knew that this was true. He was more than the Nazarene, or the enemy of the Jewish leadership, he was Jesus the Son of God.

As grief engulfed Lucius, an earthquake startled everyone on Golgotha. Then the sky began to darken. People were terrified and began to scream. Shocked by the unusual events, the crowd quickly left the hill. But, some of the leadership from Sanhedrin remained.

Lucius was disconcerted by the earthquake and the eclipse of the sun happening at the same time. He could not remember if he had experienced anything like this before. He knew what to do in a battle, civil unrest, and even in a governor's palace, but during a crucifixion an earthquake and an eclipse at the same time? Never. It was as if the earth had reacted to Jesus' death.

Looking over to the mother of Jesus and the others with her, Lucius saw how they were comforting each other. They wept and spoke softly to one another. He could not hear what they said, but he could see their broken hearts as they grieved Jesus' death. Lucius felt pain as he observed the small group.

For the next few hours, the darkness continued, as well as Lucius' knew that he had witnessed something that had come from God. Lucius monitored the guards, walked the perimeter of the hill, and looked over to the family group from time to time.

Three men of the Sanhedrin came to Lucius.

"The hour is growing late," one said. "it is nearing our Sabbath, and as Jews, we do not want anyone left on the crosses. We have permission from Pilate to have the guards break their legs."

Lucius motioned for the guards and communicated the order, then walked over to the crosses. Guards had broken the legs of the two thieves, however, the guard at Jesus' cross called out to Lucius, "He is already dead."

At first, Lucius looked up at the body of Jesus to see for himself. Jesus's head was bowed with his chin touching his chest, and his face was swollen, disfigured, and bloody. Lucius's eyes scanned the rest of his battered and broken body. It was clear that Jesus had indeed died.

Lucius felt a sorrow come over him as though it were a cloak. Waves of emotion were stirred as he viewed the sign on the top of Jesus' cross, "This is the King of the Jews." There was a sting in his eyes.

"Sir, what do you want us to do?" asked the guard.

"Pierce his side," Lucius said softly, as he continued to gaze at Jesus.

Lucius winced when he saw the guard take his spear and thrust it into the ribs of Jesus. Blood and water flowed from Jesus's side.

For a while, there was a silence, on the hill. Even the men from the Sanhedrin had stopped talking to each other.

Lucius looked at the limp body of Jesus, he asked himself the question, "What was all this for?"

Lucius was surprised by a palace guard approaching him. He began to walk toward the guard, and asked him.

"What brings you here?"

"Pilate has summoned you to the palace.," the guard announced with a salute.

"Is there a problem?"

"No, sir," the guard replied. "Pilate has a question about Jesus."

"I will leave right now," Lucius said, and he motioned for the guard to come with him.

Lucius began his walk to the palace, retracing his steps from earlier. His mind was filled with the morning's scenes on this street. He remembered, clearing the pathway for Jesus to climb the hill to his death. Lucius recalled how many were weeping for Jesus, as others shouted insults and profanity at him.

Something had changed in Lucius as he stood on that hill as he witnessed the crucifixion of Jesus. He could feel it within him as he walked into the palace. As soon as he entered, a guard took him to Pilate's chamber. Lucius was surprised that he was taken there and not to the praetorium.

Lucius solemnly greeted Pilate as he entered. He could see the stress on Pilate's face.

"Your servant sir."

"I have men asking for Jesus' body," Pilot said, getting right to the point.

"I need to know if Jesus of Nazareth is dead."

Lucius responded with some detail, "When the earth shook and the eclipse occurred,

Jesus died. He was already dead when the order came to break his legs. I had his side pierced, there was no need to break his legs."

Pilate's face was filled with sadness, brought on by Lucius' report.

"A man has requested his body, I will give permission."

Pilate then waved his hand to dismiss Lucius. It was obvious that Pilate was distressed by the day's events.

Lucius walked from the palace wondering who would ask for Jesus' body. He then began to consider where would they take him. The thoughts circled in his mind. When he returned to Golgotha, it was still quiet, there were fewer men from the Sanhedrin present.

Jesus' family group remained. They spoke quietly to each other as they comforted Mary, Jesus' mother.

Lucius gave orders to the guards to gather the tools to begin to remove the bodies from the crosses. The guards began with the two outer crosses. Lucius noticed, while the two criminals were being removed from the crosses, that two men in priestly robes arrived and went directly to the small family group. After speaking for a moment, the young man and the priests conversed with the guard.

Then the guard pointed to Lucius, and the two men walked purposefully to him. Their faces bore signs of great distress and sorrow, as they approached Lucius.

"Sir, I am Joseph of Arimathaea, this is Nicodemus, we have received permission from Pilate to take his body, and to place it in my tomb," Joseph said.

Lucius answered him with a softness in his voice, "I will have the guard assist you."

Lucius watched over the removal of Jesus from the cross. When the guard removed the nails from Jesus' hands, the lifeless body fell forward onto the shoulder of the guard. Then another guard removed the nail from his feet, completely releasing him from the cross.

The guard backed down the ladder with the body of Jesus on his shoulder.

Joseph and Nicodemus were standing at the ladder waiting. Lucius beheld the tenderness and gentleness of Joseph, and Nicodemus, as they received the lifeless body of Jesus from the guard.

Lucius knew that Joseph and Nicodemus were defying the temple leadership by their actions.

"These men are courageous." Lucius thought. "Did they believe in Jesus?"

Even though Lucius felt as though he was witnessing something so intimate, he could not turn his attention away from them. As he observed how the temple priests were handling the body of Jesus. It was with incredible care and reverence. It was clear that for them the death of Jesus was having a profound effect on them. He understood the grief of the mother, but these men were publicly contradicting the temple leadership with their work to properly bury this man.

Joseph had brought a white linen fabric to wrap Jesus's body. The cloth as placed on the ground so that the body could be placed on it. He continued to watch as Jesus' mother who was with other women near the foot of the cross. The women were doing their best to control their sorrow and anguish as they began to use the remainder of the linen fabric to wrap Jesus' body.

Not since Lucius was a child, had he felt such a lump in his throat as when he observed Jesus' mother tenderly removing the crown of thorns that had been embedded deep into his head. She then lovingly brushed the blood-encrusted hair from his swollen face. As tears streamed down and dripped from her chin, she bent over and kissed his forehead. Sitting up, she gazed at him for a moment, then took a cloth and covered his face.

She continued to sit there looking at his wrapped body, rocking slowly as she cupped a hand over her mouth.

The young man, a family member, came and . He spoke to her softly while he helped her stand. He held on to her as she began to turn slowly, She leaned heavily on him, and she covered her face with her shawl as they moved away.

The priests and women finished preparing his body. Lucius and two other guards followed at a distance as they walked slowly from Golgotha to the tomb of Joseph where Jesus would be placed. Even though the streets were crowded, many people quickly moved away from the procession. He saw the expressions of disgust and repulsion on numerous faces of the people. However, Lucius was amazed by some who openly wept as they passed by.

The hour was growing late as the sun was nearly set when they arrived in a garden and then to a tomb. Joseph carried Jesus' body inside, then Nicodemus and the young man entered as they laid Jesus down.

When the men left the tomb, Lucius motioned to the guards to help them roll the large stone over the entrance.

Lucius remained at a distance from the tomb and watched the small group. Even though his responsibility regarding Jesus was now complete, he could not leave. Something was compelling to stay.

He observed the group sitting silently near the tomb. They were watching, as if they were waiting for something, even though there was nothing that could be done. They sat and looked at the tomb, where Jesus lay. The quiet of the garden felt strange to Lucius after the hours of dealing with the crowds, the shouting people, the yelling of insults, the screams from men on the crosses, the pounding of the hammers, and the weeping.

Lucius began to feel the stress and the fatigue of the day as he stood a distance from the scene of the burial of Jesus. He knew that there was no need to stay there any longer, so he walked to the gate of the garden and onto the street and then to his quarters.

He sat at a table to write his report for Pilate. It was hard for him to believe how much had happened in just one day. The images of the day flooded his mind. He recalled when he saw Jesus being led through the streets by the Sanhedrin. Jesus was calm and unafraid. He was silent as the priests hurled insults and accusations when he stood before Pilate. However, when Pilate asked him if he was King of the Jews, he only answered "yes, it is as you say."

Lucius realized that Jesus never asked for mercy or to defend himself. Nor did he ever beg for his life. The beatings did not break him, and the cross did not crush his passion. It was as if Jesus knew exactly what was going to happen to him.

Lucius recalled each statement Jesus said from the cross. He asked his father to forgive them, because they didn't know what they were doing. He asked himself, "So, who is his father that can forgive?"

He remembered the next statement when Jesus responded to the thief who asked him to remember him in his kingdom. Jesus said to him , "Today you will be with me in paradise."

Lucius thought, "Where is this paradise? How does Jesus have authority over paradise?"

Emotion swept over him as he recalled, how from the cross, Jesus entrusted his mother to the young man to ensure her care. Jesus was mindful of the needs of his mother, as he faced his imminent death. She had trusted the young man that Jesus commanded to care for her. Countless images from Golgotha were spinning in Lucius' mind, he began to run his fingers through his hair, as if he were trying to smooth the turmoil of his thoughts.

Abruptly a vivid scene filled his mind. As it replayed, he felt the heat of the sun on the hill, the noise of the crowds, and the breeze on his face. It was when Jesus was struggling for his last breaths that Jesus spoke in a whisper, "It is finished. Into your hands, I commit my spirit."

Lucius wondered what did Jesus mean, What had he finished? What had he started? He committed his spirit to his father? Those thoughts caused him to stand suddenly and then pace the room. He continued reliving the scene. He again felt the power of the moment when at Jesus' death there was an earthquake and an eclipse.

At that moment, a spontaneous thought escaped his lips, "Surely, he is the son of God."

Lucius walked over to the large window that looked over the city, and he thought, "He must be the son of God, but now he is dead. What does that all mean?"

Lucius surveyed the silhouette of the homes of the city and saw only the glow from scattered windows across the landscape. His racing thoughts soon calmed and he began to yawn. He convinced himself that he could write the report tomorrow.

Lucius awoke to hear birds chirping and singing from his window. He was thankful that he had not been summoned to see Pilate and that there had been no serious problems through the night. He wanted to go to the tomb; something within him wanted to go there.

When he stepped out of the officer's quarters he was met with a small watch of temple guards. One guard was holding a rope and a small bucket. He explained to Lucius the chief priest and Pharisees of the temple had gone to Pilate to request that the tomb be sealed and guarded. The priests told Pilate that Jesus had told his followers, that he would be delivered into the hands of men, who would kill him. But he would rise on the third day.

The priests were afraid that Jesus' disciples would steal the body and say that Jesus had risen from the dead.

Pilate agreed to have his seal on the tomb, but the temple guards would stand watch, to ensure that no one would come and try to steal the body. Lucius nearly laughed at this, and said, "If his disciples were too afraid to be seen at Jesus' arrest and crucifixion, why would the temple leadership think that these fearful men would come and try and steal his body?"

Lucius shook his head in disgust and started walking in the direction of the garden.

"I will go to the tomb with you, as they desire."

The garden area was empty when they arrived. It was quiet. They were the only people present. The temple guards set to work on sealing the tomb. They used wax and rope, and placed in the wax the seal of Pilate.

Lucius sat on a garden bench, it was a peaceful setting. It was difficult to believe that just a few hours before he was there watching Jesus being placed in the tomb. When the guards signaled that they were done with sealing, Lucius was told that these guards were to stand watch until replacements came. The third guard returned to the priests and Pharisees to communicate that the tomb had been sealed and the guards were in place.

Lucius remained seated on the bench in the garden. Even though he was aware that he needed to return to his quarters to write the report for Pilate, there was something that held him there. His thoughts soon returned to the questions from the night before as he looked at the sealed tomb.

Immediately his thoughts returned to the many questions that he was still contemplating,"If he was the son of God, why had he come? He did not see any maliciousness within him." He continued thinking, "In fact when Jesus stood beside Barabbas on the platform before Pilate, there was an unmistakable contrast between them. There was goodness in him, he healed people and did not ask for anything in return. So why did he die?"

Again, he could not understand, yet he knew there was something important about Jesus, Lucius continued to sit in silence in the garden. After a while, he returned to his quarters to write the report for Pilate.

It was afternoon when he sent the report. He felt a relief knowing that it was all over. Since there were the temple guards at the tomb, the Jewish leadership should be satisfied. Jerusalem should return to a more normal atmosphere since Jesus was no longer a problem.

Lucius walked to the common area of the quarters and then sat at an empty table. Other men were conversing across the room. He felt restless and unsettled as he sat in the room.

Shortly, Cassius entered the room. Lucius welcomed the surprising visit and offered his cohort a seat at his table.

"I have not seen you in days, you have been in the middle of a mess here, haven't you, " Cassius said with a hint of laughter in his voice.

"You have no idea, but I think it is over.," Lucius said, running his fingers through his hair. "Then maybe I can get my transfer and I can move on. At the very least, I am due time off."

'I hope you can go to a place distant from here," Cassius responded.

"Cassius, tell me about your assignments since last we spoke?" Lucius asked hoping to talk about something else.

It felt good to talk and think about someone and something else for a while. They laughed as they shared stories of past campaigns and their experiences over the years as soldiers.

The hour was late when Cassius realized the time, he was surprised how long he had stayed with Lucius.

"I have to check on some men at the garrison. In fact, I am late now." Cassius hurried off and Lucius returned to his quarters.

Tossing and turning on the bed, Lucius had been trying to sleep for hours but sleep had not come. Night had nearly passed while his mind still was filled with the events regarding Jesus, the temple leadership, and the people.

Methodically he started at the beginning of his assignment by reevaluating each conversation he had with people in Jerusalem — the reactions of the people who had heard Jesus' messages, and the people who had witnessed Jesus heal people.

Suddenly Lucius sat up and jumped from his bed.

"How could I have forgotten?"

Lucius paced in his room back and forth, as he tried to clarify the information.

"He told me, and I forgot!"

Lucius was remembering more of the conversation as he continued to pace around the room.

"Remus! You came to me, you wanted me to know. You told me about Jesus healing your servant! Jesus healed the servant without touching or coming to your home, and he didn't ask for anything in return!"

He paced and talked as if Remus was in the room.

"You believe that Jesus is the son of God, don't you, Remus?"

At that moment, peace fell over Lucius, the turmoil left, and the agitation was gone. He stopped pacing when he stood at the window and looked out, He could see the faint light of the beginning of the sunrise to the east.

As he looked over the city, he enjoyed the calm that he felt. It was different than anything he had ever experienced. The peace stopped the spinning and the questions. Lucius took a deep breath, it was as though peace was refreshing him. He closed his eyes as he stood feeling his body relax.

Lucius walked over to his bed, laid down and then fell asleep.

Normally, Lucius was up before sunrise. He was surprised at the hour. He had slept in.

Lucius felt refreshed, as he lingered over his meal. He was thankful that he was not in a hurry to be somewhere. Again his thoughts returned to Jesus and his crucifixion as well as the conversation that Remus had with him about a week ago.

He shook his head as he contemplated the many events that had taken place, since Pilate assigned him to Jerusalem, Jesus, and the temple. Lucius had never seen the kind of hatred that the temple leadership had for Jesus and their determination to have him put to death. His mind still wrestled with questions regarding Jesus of Nazareth.

Lucius left his quarters to stretch his legs and get some fresh air. He walked down the streets of Jerusalem and then found himself at the entrance of the garden where the tomb of Jesus was located.

As Lucius approached the entrance to the garden, he was startled when he had to step aside as two men raced out. When Lucius walked to the familiar bench, he noticed that there were no guards present, and the stone was rolled away. Perplexed, he stood then looked around trying to locate the watch guards that were to be on duty, but there were none in the garden area.

Lucius then looked to and saw the tomb was open.

Hesitating for a brief moment, then approached the tomb, looked inside before he bent down to pass through the opening. Lucius' heart was beating fast. He had no idea what he was going to see, Nevertheless, he knew that something incredible had happened. Would Jesus' body still be there?

"Who rolled the stone away, he wondered. "And where are the guards?"

Lucius was not surprised that Jesus' body was not there. But, he was confused when he noticed the linen cloth that wrapped his body was folded and placed to one side. The cloth that covered his face was on the other side.

Suddenly, he then felt a presence of power and peace within the tomb. He was immediately reminded of the peace he had experienced the night before.

Determined to understand, Lucius began to analyze what he was seeing,

"If the disciples or someone came to steal his body, they would have taken it wrapped in the linen cloth," he surmised. He began to consider, "Why would the thieves take time to unwrap the body here, then steal it?"

A thought that came to mind unsettled him.

"What if Jesus rose from the dead as he had foretold?"

Lucius exited the tomb and looked around the garden again. He saw no signs of a struggle. He wondered what had happened to the temple guards?

He wanted answers, so he left the garden and decided to go to the temple to ask the chief priests and Pharisees They had placed the guards at the tomb.

Lucius arrived at the temple quickly, and he was determined to find out what happened. While Lucius looked for someone whom he could talk with, he spotted the temple guard from the day before. He motioned to him that he wanted to talk with him. The guard's expression displayed fear and hesitation as Lucius began to close the distance between them.

Lucius asked the guard, "What happened at the tomb of Jesus?"

The guard was clearly uncomfortable. answered, "Sir, you will have to talk with Caiaphas about it."

"Were you on duty this morning?" Lucius asked, as he noticed how nervous; the guard was.

"Um, please sir. You need to speak with Caiaphas, he can give you the information," the guard stammered as he inched away from Lucius.

"I can only imagine what he would tell me, but I doubt it would be the truth!" Lucius said angrily.

He was convinced that the temple leadership was hiding information. He had seen their plots and plans. As he walked toward his quarters,.

"Why were the priests and leadership doing all of this?" He remembered the numerous people that he had spoken to about Jesus., They had told him of the lame, blind, and sick people that Jesus had healed. Others had told him that Jesus' messages were about how to love and serve God, to love your neighbors, not to judge, and to forgive.

The more he remembered the more he realized that Jesus' life had an important purpose.

As he continued to walk through the streets, the frustration and anger faded from his trip to the temple. Everything from the beginning to Golgotha flooded his mind. It all began to point to a specific moment. That moment became as vivid in his mind, as it was just two days ago.

Lucius stopped walking as the magnitude of that scene replayed in his mind. It was the moment at the cross, when Jesus said, "It is finished. Father into your hands I commit my Spirit,"

He could hear himself say at that moment, "Surely, this man was the Son of God. A realization took hold of him. He had spoken the truth with that statement.

A sense of amazement and awe overwhelmed him. Lucius began again to walk toward his quarters, a smile crossed his face and then he felt hope that surprised him.

Lucius was certain that Jesus' death on the cross was Jesus's choice. It was not the doing of the Jewish leadership, Pilate, or anyone else. Jesus did not plead for his life, he did not challenge the lies of the Sanhedrin, and he did not beg for mercy from Pilate. He knew what his fate was when he was arrested.

As Lucius reflected on everything, he knew that no one had stolen Jesus' body.

Upon arriving at his quarters, Lucius knew that he was overdue for leave, so he wrote a request to Pilate for leave and then sent it by messenger. He going in the morning to look for a response.

He had a sense of excitement, as he packed his things. He was going to Capernaum, where he could learn more about Jesus.

He chuckled remembering his last encounter with Remus. He thought,"He will certainly be surprised, by what I have to tell him. I know that I have been a witness to something extraordinary. Jesus is the Son of God and he is not just for the Jews but for everyone"

Chapter 7

ETCETERA

Do you know the precise time when you surrendered your heart to Jesus, who provides all hope?

Accepting Jesus is a simple process. First you have to acknowledge that you are a sinner.

For all have sinned and fall short

of the glory of God.

Romans 3:23 ESV

You must realize that as a sinful being we will one day die.

For the wages of sin is death, but the free gift of God is eternal life in Jesus Christ our Lord.

Romans 6:23 ESV

You must believe that Jesus is the Son of God and that he gave his life that you might live.

I also received: that Christ died for our sins

in accordance with the scriptures,

that he was buried, that he was raised on the third day

in accordance with the scriptures.

1 Corinthians 15:3-4 ESV

If you believe on these things and pray for Jesus to become your lord and savior, He will accept you as a child of God, forgive you of all of your sins and give you life everlasting. You will have been born again and the Holy Spirit will indwell you.

Jesus answered, Verily, verily, I say unto thee

Except a man be born again,

he cannot see the kingdom of God

John 3:8 KJV

If you are a child of God, point others to Jesus.

The fruit of the righteous is a tree of life; and he that winneth souls is wise.

Proverbs 11:30 KJV

Glory Be to God!

Chapter 8

ABOUT THE AUTHOR

BRENDA CARROLL JARVIS is a very active Christian woman. She was a missionary in Mexico City for 17 years and after returning to the United States she started a music ministry and performed many concerts with some of the biggest names in Southern Gospel Music.

Brenda is a frequent speaker for Christian women's events. She does portrayals of Biblical women when requested. She maintains two websites: *goldenstreetsingers.com*, for her music ministry, and *Brendavotions.com*, where she posts her devotional writings and her poetry.

She has written and published three books, *Biblical Women of Influence*, *It Happened in Bethlehem* and *When My Heart Sings*. All are available from her website, *Brendavotions.com and on Amazon*.

Brenda enjoys sharing her faith wherever the Lord leads her. Often, she will pray with or encourage people via telephone. It is Brenda's passion that everyone understands the great gift in salvation, the power of God's unlimited love and the transformational grace through Jesus Christ.

She grew up in Fort Wayne, IN, but now resides in the summers in a Civil War-era farmhouse in Farmdale, OH, and the winters in a coastal-area cottage in Brunswick, GA.